Ian MacKintosh

Warship

from the BBC television series
devised by
Ian MacKintosh & Anthony Coburn

ARROW BOOKS

ARROW BOOKS LTD

3 Fitzroy Square, London W1

AN IMPRINT OF THE HUTCHINSON GROUP

London Melbourne Sydney Auckland
Wellington Johannesburg Cape Town
and agencies throughout the world

First published 1973

*Made and printed in Great Britain
by The Anchor Press Ltd,
Tiptree, Essex*
ISBN 0 09 907740 X

WARSHIP

*

A signal in the night sends HMS *Hero* racing into the Caribbean, to the aid of a ditched airliner. Only when the frigate is committed to rushing the survivors to hospital on the island of Mongada does *Hero*'s captain, Mark Nialls, learn that the airliner was sabotaged and that Mongada, strife-torn by an impending presidential election, is a stronghold for the saboteurs.

The situation brings new tests for Derek Beaumont, Bob Last, Pat Fuller and the rest of *Hero*'s company as Nialls is drawn into a struggle which becomes intensely personal as well as violently political.

To

ANTHONY COBURN

friend, taskmaster
and mentor extraordinary

Contents

AUTHOR'S NOTE

Although Tony Coburn and I created the main characters and the essential storylines for the *Warship* series, neither of us would wish to minimise in any way the immense contribution made to the whole format by the other writers and the directors. It is appropriate for me, therefore, to record here our thanks to them all for the privilege and pleasure of scheming with them.

In no particular order of beauty or seniority, we acknowledge gratefully the connivance of:

Donald Bull	Robert Holmes
Frank Cox	Lennie Mayne
David Cunliffe	Alun Richards
Stuart Douglass	John Wiles
Mervyn Haisman	Martin Worth
Manus Hardy	

I.M.

I

Divert with Dispatch

Predictably, monotonously, the bows dipped into the dark Caribbean and then rose again; proudly shaking off the sea in an impatient flurry of spray that whipped shimmering and solid out of the night to hammer back at the bridge windows. The wipers fought a brief encounter and, for a moment or two, the windows were clear.

Not, Mark Nialls thought, hunched in the captain's chair, that there was anything to see. The night was such that the warm, sunny day which had preceded it was already a memory. This was a winter night, starless and cheerless and foreboding, hanging like an undertaker's umbrella over a cold, restless, hungry ocean. An ocean into which, three hours before—just on midnight local time—one hundred and nine souls had been pitched from a ditching airliner.

Men, women, children. Praying, cursing, crying. Swimming, drowning, dying. How many of them could still be alive?

It was, Nialls knew, an academic question; and a futile one. HMS *Hero* was doing more than thirty knots for the crash position. She could go no faster; there was nothing more to be done before they got there, in about forty minutes' time.

He lit a cigarette and leaned back in the chair, unconsciously stressing himself against the movement of the frigate as it battered and corkscrewed its way through the head sea. So much for the gentle, uneventful passage to Jamaica that was supposed to have succeeded the past three weeks of hard exercising in the western Atlantic with units of the United States Navy.

He stretched out a hand and lifted the yeoman's clipboard, on top of which was the signal that had changed their plans and abruptly turned their thoughts from dreams of Planter's Punch and Caribbean Christmas shopping. It said:

FLASH. UNCLASSIFIED. FROM MINISTRY OF DEFENCE (NAVY) TO HMS HERO. INFORMATION COMMANDER-IN-CHIEF WESTERN ATLANTIC AREA, COMMANDER-IN-CHIEF FLEET AND SENIOR NAVAL OFFICER WEST INDIES.

BRITISH FEDERATED AIRWAYS BOEING 707 ON FLIGHT LONDON TO KINGSTON CRASHED IN APPROXIMATE POSITION 24°37′N 70°29′W AT 2358 LOCAL TIME. LAST MESSAGE FROM CAPTAIN INDICATED EXPLOSION, ON FIRE AND ATTEMPTING DITCHING. SEA STATE IN AREA IS FORCE EIGHT. AIRCRAFT REPORTED CARRYING NINETY-NINE PASSENGERS AND TEN CREW. DIVERT WITH UTMOST DISPATCH TO PICK UP SURVIVORS. REPORT ESTIMATED TIME OF ARRIVAL IN RESCUE AREA.

Later had come a more accurate position from an American long-range maritime patrol aircraft, which had dropped twenty-man liferafts over the winking fireflies of light from the lifebelts of survivors—or bodies—in the sea, and the news that the American liner *Tarrametta* was also racing to the scene, with an estimated arrival time only fifty minutes behind that of *Hero*. Nialls had exchanged signals with the *Tarrametta*'s master and had been promised the services of a doctor—from among the liner's passengers—as soon as the *Tarrametta* was within range of *Hero*'s Wasp helicopter.

It would be no easy matter winching up the doctor from the liner, in the dark and in this wind and sea, and then landing again on the frigate's tiny, pitching flight deck; but it did not cross Nialls' mind to question the ability of his flight commander, Lieutenant Peter Boswall, to achieve the transfer. Boswall was a member of the team, and the team had proved many times before that it could react speedily and efficiently to any emergency.

In this instance, the ship's company had swung into action with quiet, grim and determined effort. It reminded Nialls of a time in the Mediterranean when they had responded with similar dispatch to an S O S from a stricken submarine. There was the same mood about them, the same understated resolve and fixity of purpose, the same concern and compassion that belied their normal outward appearance of tough, go-lucky individuals who were content to play the world with studied disdain and to impromptu rules.

The wardroom, his own and the officers' cabins

and all messdecks with easy access from the upper deck had been quickly prepared as receiving stations, the sick bay had become a nerve-centre of activity, the galley crews were ready to serve soups, tea and coffee, the stores ratings had brought up extra blankets, all boats had been checked and crews detailed, jumping ladders were rigged, extra lookouts had been briefed, searchlights were resited, the Wasp was at immediate readiness.

Much of this was due, Nialls knew, to the calm and seemingly effortless organising ability of his first lieutenant, Derek Beaumont. At thirty-four, Beaumont was only two years younger than Nialls; but Nialls was a commander, and Beaumont a lieutenant-commander. And there were those who said that Derek Beaumont lacked the flair and imagination to be promoted. But now, when the chips were down, Beaumont had all the answers and most of the ideas.

Nialls turned to look to the back of the darkened bridge, and to the chart-table where Beaumont was in soft-toned conversation with Lieutenant Bob Last, the navigating officer. And not for the first time, Nialls realised how lucky he was to have these two. Last, twenty-six and a bachelor like Beaumont, was a born seaman and a brilliant navigator with a brain that could computerise such factors as wind, tide, distance, speed and sea conditions and put the ship in a stated place at a stated time with unerring accuracy. And it could be, this bleak Wednesday morning, that Last's ability to bring the ship to a pinpoint in an ocean would save lives and alleviate suffering.

Nialls hoped so, with every fibre of his being.

Fiona Hunt felt the relentless cold seep to every fibre of *her* being, through the saturated tunic of her blue stewardess' uniform and her equally sodden and unsubstantial underclothing. Sea-water slopped across the floor of the liferaft—having smashed its way in, despite the canopy and side-screens—and washed icily around her as she fought for balance against the craft's tossing and plunging. Then she knelt again at the side of the elderly woman.

In the torchlight, the lined old face was deathly white and there was an oddly pathetic quality about the incongruity of yellow lifejacket, pink twinset and pearls, such that tears pricked at the back of Fiona's blue eyes and sorrow tugged at her already-frayed emotions. For the woman was dying.

It seemed so unfair. To have survived the horror of the crash, the terror of being hurled into a black and hostile sea, only to have an old frame and a tired heart surrender to the double-blow of exposure and shock. To live, say, seventy years; to embark on a Great Adventure to the sun (*with B.F.A. the West Indies are as easy as the West End*); and then to die in this small rubber boat, far from friends and home and in the undistinguished company of a frightened and ineffectual stewardess— and she *was* frightened, Fiona admitted to herself with a sense of shame—and a man who was even more frightened and, in their current predicament, even more ineffectual.

Fiona glanced across at him. She could see little

of him, in the darkness, but she knew that he was fifty, fat and fearful now that the crash and the motion of the raft had wrung from him the alcoholic euphoria that had been the basis of his bombast and self-esteem in the aircraft. Now, the raft stank of his sickness and echoed—even above the noise of the wind and sea—to his constant complaints. He addressed Fiona still as 'stewardess', in a tone which made clear that she was considered a serving-girl and no fit companion, even in these circumstances, for Archibald Gorme-Critchley.

Fiona turned back from him, took the cold, wrinkled hand of the woman and bent to the grey hair. She asked: 'Are you awake, Mrs Buchan?'

'Yes, my dear.' The voice was as frail as the hand, and failing. 'But I can't stop shivering. I can't . . .'

'Just hang on,' soothed Fiona. 'There'll be ships coming to us from all directions. We'll soon be tucked up in warm beds.'

'Stewardess!' This voice was hoarse—Fiona recalled that she had found Critchley screaming for help—and edged with hysteria. 'What're you saying, girl? What?'

'I was saying,' Fiona shouted, 'that there will be ships on the way to us. We should be picked up soon.'

'Bloody fool child!' Critchley broke off to spit revoltingly as vomit rose in his throat. 'Don't you know *anything*? Damned ship could pass a hundred yards away in this weather, never see us! Too stupid to realise the danger you've put us in! Bloody incompetence and bad maintenance. Fool pilots. Stupid stewardesses and . . .' The mumbling became incoherent. Then, sharply: 'Disgrace! Damn . . .'

'There was an explosion!' Fiona retorted. 'You may have been too drunk to remember, Mr Critchley, but there was an explosion in the baggage compartment. Then a fire. Captain Curtis had no choice but to try to ditch the aeroplane. In a very rough sea. And he saved at least some of us. Including *you*, Mr Critchley. You've a lot to be thankful for!'

'Gorme-Critchley. And remember your place, young woman. Drunk. Drunk indeed! Might have been a chance if the service hadn't been so bloody awful. Worst airline I ever . . .'

'Oh, shut up!' snapped Fiona.

'Dare you!' Critchley spat again. 'Insolence! Have you reported!'

'Now,' Fiona injected warmth into her tone, 'that's more like it! You're beginning to have faith in our being picked up!'

'Bitch,' Critchley said. But he lapsed to silence.

Fiona closed her eyes, stilled her own shivering and lifted Mrs Buchan into her arms, trying to impart what little body-heat she had into the desperately thin and shaking old lady. Perhaps, Fiona thought, if I can keep her alive, I won't feel so bad.

But the nagging doubt persisted. Maybe Critchley was right. Maybe she *was* incompetent. Critchley could not know that this was her first flight as a qualified stewardess. And she did not know if she had been right—if she had *had* the right—to climb into this raft as soon as she had come upon it. Should she have remained in the water, in her lifejacket, to look for other people; perhaps children? There *had* been children on the flight. What had happened to them? What had happened to the other stewardesses? The flight deck crew?

The trouble was that none of this had occurred to her until after she was in comparative safety, aboard the raft. And then, she had not had the courage to override the survival-instinct and return again to that cold and vicious sea outside.

God, but she had been afraid when the Boeing hit the sea! The aircraft had cracked in two, like an eggshell, just abaft the wing-roots. She had had time to unbelt, get to her feet and then . . . and then the sea had rushed in, and sucked her away into the churning, kaleidoscopic confusion of the night. Tossing on a wave-top, she had seen the for'ard end of the Boeing slide beneath the surface. No doubt, the tail section had gone, too. And with it, too many souls; too many poor people, perhaps still awaiting an order, a word from a stewardess no longer there.

She had been so proud, last week, to abandon teenage, celebrate her twentieth birthday and re-ceive her stewardess' wings, on the same day. And two days after that, she had become engaged to be married. She had felt so grown-up, so responsible, so collected.

And now. And now . . .

'Clothes?' queried Able Seaman Regard, standing defensively in front of his locker.

'Clothes,' confirmed Leading Regulator Pat

Fuller, as if to an idiot. 'Warm clothes. I'm collecting.'

'I've given some,' Regard said, pointing to the messdeck table. 'My spare set of working dress.'

'I see.' Fuller lifted the blue denim shirt off the table, holding it at arm's length by two fingers. 'Dirty,' he commented. 'And holed. I reckon you must be about due for a kit-muster.'

'All I got,' Regard insisted, staring up into the suspicious Scots face of Fuller, who was known onboard as 'the sheriff' and had a habit of conducting his enquiries on messdecks with all the gusto and dedication of Wyatt Earp on the streets of Tombstone.

'Can I open your locker?' requested Fuller, reaching at the same time behind Regard and snapping it open. 'Ah, that's more like it!'

He extracted a bright red, heavy woollen sweater and shook it out on the table. 'Very kind of you.'

'Here, Sheriff!' Regard was horrified. 'That's new! Almost. It's a . . . oh, all right then. I suppose it's in a good cause.'

'Stop some dolly's bum from freezing,' Fuller agreed cheerfully. 'Now, who's got a pair of long Johns?'

On the bridge, Bob Last was adjusting the ship's course to find an acceptable wind over the deck for the helicopter's return.

'Starboard ten.'

'Starboard ten.' The quartermaster's voice came back to him over the loudspeaker, from the wheelhouse three decks below. 'Ten of starboard wheel on, sir.'

'Very good.' Last's eyes went to the compass repeater tape. 'How are you managing to hold her in this sea, quartermaster?'

'Can't manage better than two degrees either side, sir.'

'All right. Do your best. The flight commander can always change his trousers when he gets onboard.'

In his chair, Nialls smiled faintly around a cigarette. It was a pleasure to watch Last at work; superbly confident, relaxed and with the total awareness that marks all great seamen, Last could step in and take over from an officer of the watch—in this case, another lieutenant—without question or rancour. Yet he did so now, Nialls knew, not to impress his captain, but because he could put the ship on the correct course in the shortest time, settle the quartermaster and be totally prepared—with scope to double-check—before the difficult Wasp landing. Peter Boswall, battling his helicopter back to the ship, would be grateful to know that his welfare was in Last's hands. And, of course, in the hands of Monty Wakelin.

Wakelin was on the flight deck, sheltering just inside the hangar door as he tested the hand-torches with which he would 'bat' Boswall to the deck. A thirty-year-old lieutenant, Wakelin was the senior flight deck officer, although primarily the ship's supply officer and head of the supply department: an hour before, he had been around his storerooms and galleys, talking in terms of blankets and beverages; now, he was more concerned with wind speeds and deck pitch. It was, he thought for the thousandth time, a change of character that would have been envied by Dr Jekyll.

And thinking of doctors, he hoped that this one coming in from the liner had a strong heart and a steady nerve: it was hard enough to make oneself believe that the Wasp could get on to this tiny pocket-handkerchief of flight deck in daylight; to see the size of landing area for the first time at night, in a force eight gale and from the business end, demanded an iron constitution and a philosophical nature. If the incoming passenger had not been endowed with both, the sick bay's first patient this morning could be a very shaken doctor.

But, in fact, the sick bay's first patient that morning was Able Seaman Regard. Being idle by nature, Regard had taken some time to get round to closing his locker after the leading regulator's visit and when, finally, he had been moved to do so (because assorted articles had started to fall out of it), he had chosen the precise moment in which Last had ordered the alteration of course. The ship had lurched, the locker door had swung smartly shut and Regard's fingers had acted as an unwilling but highly effective door-stop.

Now, Leading Medical Assistant Peters stood back to admire his artistry with Elastoplast.

'You'll live,' he pronounced at length.

'Thanks, Doc,' returned Regard.

'Don't call me "Doc" this morning,' Peters said testily, gathering up his medical satchel and making for the door. 'We've got a real doctor coming onboard in a minute. And I've got to get to flying stations before he does.'

Regard crinkled his brow. The day was already too much for him. He protested: 'I've always called you "Doc". Everybody calls you "Doc". Even the first lieutenant.'

'But not when we've got a real doctor onboard, you dummy. Especially a civvy doctor. It would be an affront to him.'

Regard's brow stayed crinkled. 'What are you, then?'

'I'm an L.M.A. Even you should . . .'

'I know that, Doc! I mean—what are you to the civvy, like?'

'I'm a combination of a male nurse, a hospital orderly and . . .'

'Oh,' Regard smiled, beating Peters to the door. 'Well, thank you, Nurse. We'll have to have a party when you get rated up to Sister!'

Peters' eyes narrowed as he watched Regard flee up the passage, then he grinned and shrugged his shoulders. It was as well that the youngsters like Regard should be able to joke in these last few minutes before they reached the search area. It was going to be a harrowing time for them all, and a day that would stay with them for the rest of their lives.

The doctor materialised as a small, wiry American in his late forties, with an iron-grey crew-cut and bright brown eyes. He introduced himself as John Almanna and endeared himself to Nialls when he cut across the welcoming banter on the bridge and asked that he be taken to the sick bay at once.

A worthy member of the team, Nialls thought. And again, that he was lucky. If only, now, the luck would hold for those in the sea.

He looked across at Derek Beaumont. 'Number One, make sure that the Wasp is turned around as quickly as possible. Maximum fuel. Crewman with a searchlight. Take off again as soon as they can make it and into the search area to vector us on to anything they find.'

'Aye, aye, sir.' Beaumont had, in fact, already given the same orders to the flight deck, and he knew that Nialls would have so expected. Nialls was merely thinking aloud, checking off a mental list, keying himself to the task ahead.

Beaumont was about to leave the bridge when the yeoman, appearing from the gloom on the starboard side, announced: 'Flash signal from M.O.D., sir.'

'Read it,' instructed Nialls—had it been a message for his eyes only, Yeoman Dick Dancer would have simply placed it in his hand. Dancer, too, was a member of the team.

The signal said:

ALTHOUGH YOU SHOULD CONCENTRATE ON PICK-ING UP SURVIVORS, IT WOULD BE APPRECIATED IF YOU COULD ADDITIONALLY COLLECT AND PRE-SERVE AS MUCH WRECKAGE AS POSSIBLE FOR ANALYTICAL PURPOSES. MESSAGE IN SIMILAR TERMS GOES TO TARRAMETTA.

'I was wondering about that,' Nialls said, to the bridge in general. 'An explosion could mean sabotage. But our primary concern is to save life and recover bodies.' And to Beaumont: 'Don't let them get too obsessed with gathering bits and pieces. Not if they've got people in the boats.'

'Right, sir.' Beaumont made a mental note to tell the master-at-arms that there were to be no souvenir collections, either: every fragment of the aircraft might hold a clue for the experts.

'Yeoman,' Nialls' mind was still in top gear, 'I want an organisation for getting names of survivors and names or details of bodies back to the M.O.D. as fast as we can. And tell your lads to take great care over it. No mistakes. There'll be a lot of anxious people in England this morning.'

In Northwood, Middlesex, it was already a crisp, bright morning and Sir Donald Lampton, the Commander-in-Chief Fleet, was donning his admiral's uniform in his dressing-room at Admiralty House. He reached a hand to a table and to his radio, and the sound came up on a news bulletin: '... the crash occurred at two minutes to five Greenwich Mean Time this morning and as yet, there is no news of survivors. First ship on the scene should be the Royal Navy frigate HMS *Hero*, now reported to be racing through darkness and heavy seas to the crash position. HMS *Hero*, a modern frigate of the Leander Class, is fully equipped to deal with emergencies and a doctor is being transferred to the ship from the American liner *Tarrametta*, which is also making full speed to search for survivors. At their Heathrow headquarters, a spokesman for British Federated Airways said . . .'

The admiral switched off the radio and buttoned his jacket, flicking imaginary specks of dust from the lapels. He knew already of the crash, having been telephoned in accordance with his standing orders by the duty operations officer, and he reflected now—as he had done at the time of that initial report—that he was glad that Nialls had won the job. *Hero* was a good ship, well led and equal to the task; daunting though that might be.

He wondered absently, checking his tie in a long wall mirror, how long it would be before Mark Nialls shipped an admiral's uniform. Sooner than most, he was sure: there was no doubt in his own mind that Nialls was going places fast.

And so, of course, was *Hero*. And that was the immediate concern.

Oh God, prayed the admiral, let them be in time.

'Bridge, Helicopter Control Officer.' On a loud-speaker from the Operations Room below. 'Wasp reports now over a large raft. Bearing two-six-six, twelve point five miles.'

'Steer two-six-six,' rapped Nialls.

'Course *is* two-six-six, sir,' replied the officer of the watch.

Nialls half-smiled and swivelled to look at his navigating officer, at the chart-table.

'That must be about four cans of beer I owe you now, Pilot.'

'Fourteen, sir,' Last amended. He went to the

main broadcast microphone. 'Warn the ship's company, sir?'

'I'll take it,' Nialls nodded. And into the microphone: 'D'ye hear there? Captain speaking. We are now entering the search zone and the Wasp has reported sighting at least one raft. All hands stand by. Anyone seeing anything of the remotest possible interest is to report the fact to the bridge at once. Remember that lives are at stake. Nothing is too small or too insignificant to be investigated this morning.' He paused. 'It's not going to be pleasant for any of us. It's going to be dirty, difficult, dangerous. It's going to be sickening, and probably heart-breaking. But we must work quickly, and we must work well. Now, go to it. And good luck.'

'Amen,' muttered Dancer, from the bridge wing. He looked out and down to the surface of the sea; black but white-capped and restless in its cruel, callous passage across the face of the night.

'Amen,' he said again.

2

A Long Night

'Papa Bravo,' Boswall said into his throat-mike, calling *Hero*, 'this is four-seven-one.'

'Go ahead, four-seven-one,' in his earphones.

'This is four-seven-one. I am now over an uninflated raft. Appears to be the body of a child on top of it. In danger of being washed off. Over.'

'Roger, four-seven-one. Your position marked. Will be investigated.'

'Roger and out.' Boswall turned the Wasp and moved slowly into a sweep to the west. His heart was leaden. A twenty-five-year-old short-service officer, he had joined the Navy for the joy of learning to fly, had come to love it and since joining *Hero* had been involved in numerous adventures. But nothing, nothing ever like this.

It would have been bad enough in daylight and in a calm sea. In these conditions, it was a nightmare. Wreckage, bodies, belongings floated into the pool of his crewman's searchlight for a brief and tantalising moment—just long enough to report them——and then the sea-pattern changed and they disappeared again. And at the same time, he was trying to keep a concerned eye on the fate of the ship's boats as they reared and plunged to the bucketing and bidding of wind and sea.

Sensibly—thanks, presumably, to the foresight of Beaumont's briefing—the boats had not attempted to get alongside manned rafts, but had passed lines and taken them in tow to the ship. At least, that was what had happened to the two rafts which Boswall had seen. A mere two. Even if they had been crammed to the gunwales, he thought, they could not have contained more than fifty people between them.

In fact, the rafts had contained only ten people: three (Fiona Hunt, Mrs Buchan and Critchley) in one, and seven in the other. In this latter, there had been the aircraft's senior steward, three male passengers, two women and a girl of eight. One other man had been found alive but unconscious in his life-jacket and the rest of the grim total, so far, amounted to eleven bodies, including that of a stewardess, and the near-decapitated corpse of a young West Indian woman. The *Tarrametta*, only recently on the scene, could add only another two males— both dead.

Twenty-five, Nialls thought, from a total of one hundred and nine. And how many of those eleven living would remain alive without hospitalisation? He leaned forward in his chair, unhooked the main broadcast microphone and spoke into it. 'D'ye hear there? Captain speaking. I would be grateful if any members of the aircraft's crew who are fit enough to do so would report to me on the bridge after medical attention.'

And in the sick bay, Fiona Hunt—now dressed in a pair of blue action-working-dress trousers and Regard's sweater—told Peters: 'I feel all right, now. Shall I go to the bridge?'

'Yes please, miss.' Then, to a seaman: 'Frimley, take the young lady up to the captain.'

'O.K., Doc,' acknowledged Frimley, winning a glare from Peters and sudden interest from Critchley, who was sitting on the desk, playing nervously with the neckband of a borrowed seaman's jersey.

'Are you a doctor?' Critchley asked of Peters, taking in the blue open-necked shirt and leading hand's anchor badge.

'No, sir. I'm a leading rating in the medical branch. Now, let's have a look at you and we'll get you off to a bed somewhere.' Peters put his fingers to Critchley's wrist and Critchley snatched his arm away.

Peters grimaced. 'I'd like to take your pulse, sir. Just as a precaution.'

'I want to see the doctor.'

'Well, sir,' Peters glanced to where Dr Almanna was tending Mrs Buchan and the unconscious man, both of whom were now in the sick bay cots, 'the doctor's busy, as you can see. But you look to be in pretty good shape. I'll try your pulse and your temperature and if you're still ticking at the right rate,' a smile, 'we'll organise another coffee and a bunk for you.'

'Look, you fool,' Critchley hissed, 'I've been in the *sea*. Can't you get that through your thick head?'

Peters kept his smile. 'Oh indeed, sir. But my

point is that we have some rather ill people here, and the doctor must attend to them first. You *are* feeling . . . reasonably all right, aren't you?'

'I want a thorough check-up. From the doctor.'

Peters stared at him, in amazement and disbelief. 'What?'

'I've been in an air-crash. Shock. Cold. I want a check-up. Now. I'm not National Health, you know!'

'We don't have National Health in the Navy, sir.' Peters, normally the mildest of men, was having difficulty in controlling even his slow temper. 'We work on the basis that those in most need come first. And that puts you at the back of the queue this morning, sir. Later on in the day, if it's at all possible, you'll get your check-up. But you've nothing to worry about at the moment. You're warm, safe and a good rest will sort you out completely. There's a signal gone off to London to say that you've been rescued, so you're all right on that score, too. Your wife'll know very soon.'

'I'm not married.'

'I'm not surprised,' Peters said under his breath. And more audibly: 'If you'd like to go with Leading Writer Parkins, he'll . . .'

'I'll go when I'm ready!'

'Sir,' Peters was now grim-faced and flat-voiced, 'I'll take your pulse and your temperature if you wish, but then . . .'

'Don't be insolent!' Critchley thundered. 'I'll have you reported. I have friends in the Navy. In high places. I . . .'

'If you don't shut up,' Derek Beaumont said,

from the sick bay doorway, 'you'll need a friend
in the highest place of all. Because I'll take you on
to the upper deck and kick you back over the side.
As long as you're a passenger in this ship, you'll
take orders from Naval personnel as and when they
are given.'

Critchley blinked. 'Who the hell are you?'

'I'm the first lieutenant and second-in-command.'
Beaumont turned to the leading writer, who was
enjoying the moment. 'Parkins, take this gentleman
to the senior ratings' dining hall, offer him a drink
and a meal and then allocate a bunk for him. And
turn him in, even if you have to tie him to it!'

In the captain's day cabin, Nialls was seated opposite Fiona Hunt and the Boeing's senior steward, a
thin, hollow-cheeked and balding man with his left
arm in one of Doc Peters' slings.

'So what you're saying, Mr Bayldon,' Nialls sum-
marised, 'is that not many *would* have got out?'

'I don't think so, sir. I saw the tail go under. It
had filled with water. I . . .' he swallowed, 'I'm afraid
a lot of them would have been . . . drowned in their
seats.'

Nialls looked now to the stewardess. Not even
the rigours of the night, he thought absently, could
mar that kind of beauty. Very fair hair, blue eyes
in a delicate, alluring face. And so very young.

'Miss Hunt,' gently, 'I'm sorry to take you
through it again. But is there anything you can
add?'

'No, sir. I saw the for'ard section go. It was the
same. I doubt if the flight deck crew had a chance.'

'The flight deck crew? You mean the captain, the pilots?'

'Yes.' There was a tremble in Fiona's lower lip. 'We carried a captain, first officer, flight engineer, flight navigator, the senior steward here and . . . five stewardesses.'

'And ninety-nine passengers?'

'That's correct,' Bayldon nodded. 'I remember the check.'

'Right.' Nialls offered his cigarette-box. Fiona took one; Bayldon declined. 'And what about the explosion?' Nialls was putting a light to Fiona's cigarette, then his own. 'London have been asking for details.'

Bayldon nodded again. 'It was in the hold. Quite a big bang. Then smoke. Then flames. A real fire.'

Nialls drew on his cigarette as his mind, almost against his will, conjured up the horror of it. A huge, mighty jet, powered by four healthy Pratt and Whitney engines, moving majestically and imperiously through the sky. Warm, secure, unchallengeable. The pretty stewardesses, in their yellow smocks and white blouses, serving drinks and dinner. All thoughts on bright sun and Caribbean beaches.

Then fire.

And nowhere to go. Except down. Down into a sea that, in an instant, could break the back of the proud Boeing and strip it of its majesty. Down, in a screaming, whimpering huddle of doomed humanity.

They had been through a great deal, these two.

'Do you think,' he queried softly, 'that it was a bomb?'

'I couldn't say, sir.' Bayldon's tone matched Nialls'. 'It sounded like it. But you never know. We have lists of prohibited articles, but passengers carry all sorts of things. I wouldn't like to . . .'

He broke off to a knock on the door, and Beaumont came in. 'Excuse me, sir. Dr Almanna is concerned about three of the patients. Particularly an old woman who's suffering from shock and hypothermia. He thinks that we should break off as soon as we can and make for the nearest large hospital. He . . .'

'You can't abandon the search before daylight!' Fiona reacted. Then: 'I'm sorry, Captain. I . . .'

'Not at all, Miss Hunt.' Nialls smiled to the lovely face, and felt himself caught in the enchantment of the blue, fathomless eyes. 'Exactly my own objection. We'll have to balance every factor very carefully.' He lifted the microphone at his side. 'Bridge, Captain. Is the navigator there?'

'Here, sir.' Last's voice.

'Pilot, where would be the nearest large hospital?'

'Just had a signal on that, sir. Yeoman brought it to me first because he'd never heard of the place mentioned in it. M.O.D. say they have diplomatic clearance for us to put into Mongada. That's a small independent island about a hundred and twenty miles due north of the Caicos. About the same distance, too, from present position; roughly, southwest.'

'Hospital there?'

'Very good one, sir. British built and British and French staffed. I remember reading about it. The local president is one of those rare birds who's actually used aid-monies on schools and hospitals.'

'Good.' Nialls hesitated and glanced at Fiona Hunt, before continuing: 'What's the tally now, Pilot?'

'We've recovered another three bodies, sir. All female passengers. And *Tarrametta*'s picked up one male passenger who's still alive and apparently in reasonable shape. They've also collected quite a lot of wreckage.' A pause from Last. Then: 'New signal, sir. A team of air accident investigators will be flying to Mongada to make initial investigations and interview survivors. Ah . . . grateful if we will take all available pieces of wreckage, for delivery to them.'

'Roger. Ask the *Tarrametta* for her intentions.'

'Aye aye, sir.'

'And, Pilot . . . bring the Wasp back on. Don't take any arguments from Boswall, tell him he's to have at least thirty minutes' rest and he's to report to me in person for approval to take off again.'

'Aye aye, sir. Engineer officer's here, sir. He would like to come down to see you.'

'Very good. Ask him to come down now.' Nialls placed the microphone back on its wall-hook, then smiled to Fiona and Bayldon. 'We'll signal London with the details of what happened. I think you should both turn in. We'll call you if there's anything you should know or be consulted on.'

'Captain,' Fiona spoke slowly, 'if you don't mind, I'd rather stay up for the present.'

'So would I, sir.' Bayldon managed a brief, embarrassed smile. 'We don't have to explain to you two gentlemen that . . . well, we feel we have a duty.'

'I understand.' Nialls got to his feet with them. 'You're welcome to go to the bridge. Or we can put a cabin at your disposal.'

'I'd prefer to go back to the sick bay,' Fiona said.

Bayldon nodded concurrence. 'We may be able to help the doctor.'

'All right. Tell him that I'll break off as soon as I can and go flat out for that hospital in Mongada.' He nodded to Beaumont to stay, then opened the door for Fiona and Bayldon, to reveal the engineer officer in battered, oil-stained cap and once-white overalls. 'Come in, Chief.'

Jack Junnion, the engineer officer, stepped into the cabin and grinned tiredly at Beaumont. A little older than Beaumont, and a lieutenant-commander, Jack Junnion was a sound, cheerful officer whose love-hate relationship with his engines dominated his life. He asked: 'How's it going, Derek?'

'We haven't found very many of them,' Beaumont admitted. 'And fewer alive. I'm glad those two made it, though,' indicating to the door. 'Steward and stewardess. Damned fine advertisement for their airline.'

'I agree,' Nialls said, closing the door. 'What's your trouble, Chief?'

Junnion grimaced. 'I'm sorry to compound your problems, sir. But the port engine didn't like all that time at full speed.'

Nialls scratched at the beginnings of a beard. 'I'm going to ask for *more* time at full speed, I'm afraid. Can I have it?'

'Where are we going, sir?'

'An island called . . . Mongada. About one hundred and twenty miles away.'

'Four hours, say.' Junnion thought for a moment. 'O.K., sir. We can botch-job it for four hours, but I'll need three or four days in harbour when we get there.'

'Fine,' Nialls nodded. 'We'll ask M.O.D. for extended diplomatic clearance. There's going to be an aircraft investigation thing there, anyway. Expect we'll have to give evidence to that. Do you know yet what the trouble is?'

'Not really. We'll have to shut down for that. Over-heating in various places. *And* the main feed pump's shaking itself to bits. But we'll cope, even if we have to . . .'

'Captain, sir, Navigating Officer,' from the loudspeaker.

Nialls lifted the microphone. 'Yes, Pilot?'

'*Tarrametta* says she's placed herself under your orders. She's content to remain in the search area for longer, if we wish to proceed to Mongada, but would like to head for the States when released and to transfer survivors, bodies and wreckage to us before we go.'

'She's no seriously ill survivors, has she?'

'None, sir.'

'Very well. How long is it since we recovered a body?'

'Ah . . . twenty-three minutes, sir.'

'Right. Immediate to M.O.D., Commander-in-Chief Fleet and S.N.O.W.I. "Intend to break off search at first light and proceed best speed to Mongada with all survivors, bodies and wreckage recovered. Survivors include very seriously ill patients. Will leave *Tarrametta* to continue search until midday local or as decided by her master in light prevailing circumstances. *Tarrametta* will proceed direct U.S.A. unless finding survivor requiring immediate hospitalisation at Mongada." Add an estimated time of arrival in Mongada for us, and request any necessary extension of dipclear to enable us to remain three days for repair of engine defects. Something like that. Got it?'

'Yes, sir.'

Nialls replaced the microphone. 'Happy, Chief?'

'Let's say, less miserable, sir.' Junnion picked up his cap. 'I'll get back to the battle.'

'Good luck.' Nialls went to his desk and took a pen and a signal pad. 'I'd better draft a message to London on what Bayldon and Miss Hunt told me about the crash.'

Beaumont raised an eyebrow. 'Sabotage, sir?'

'Can't be ruled out.' Nialls looked up into the drawn face of his first lieutenant. 'You've had a rough morning, haven't you?'

Beaumont nodded. 'It's been tough. I've seen things today I won't forget in a long time. Like Able Seaman Adge—the big three-badge-man in the gunners' mess—coming up a jumping-ladder from a boat with the body of a two-year-old boy in his arms. He's a tough old bird, is Adge. He's seen it all. But there were tears in his eyes, and I wanted to weep, too.'

'Have you changed the boats' crews?'

'Yes, sir. After an argument. Everyone wants to be involved. To have something positive to do.'

'I doubt there's much more they can do, now. Except to pray that we get to Mongada in time to save those we've got.' Nialls shook his head. 'It's been a long night, Derek, and I won't be sorry to see the dawn.'

By the time dawn was fully upon them, Beaumont had recalled and hoisted all boats, Boswall had made a last and fruitless sweep of the area and Nialls had reported the final tally, having taken all *Tarra-metta*'s finds, of thirteen alive and twenty-one dead. Lucky thirteen, he thought. And let it so remain for them, and reward for Dr Almanna—who had elected to stay with *Hero* until Mongada and fly home from there.

Nialls kept to the bridge until the ship had worked up to full speed, on course for Mongada, then re-tired to his cabin to change from night clothing to fresh white shirt and shorts. He was tired, but no more tired—he knew—than the two hundred and sixty other men in his ship's company. And a good deal less tired than Boswall, Last, Beaumont, Dr Almanna, Peters and the boats' crews. But it was pointless to tell Last to get off the bridge, or order Beaumont to relax and cease his constant patrolling of the ship; encouraging here, chiding there, keep-ing the team together. As always, they had met the challenge superbly and . . .

There was a knock on the door and the communications officer came in, to place a signal on the table before him. Nialls read it quickly, knowing even before he had seen the marking on it of *Exclusive Top Secret* that it was important and sensitive: had it been of lesser significance, it would not have required decryption from the special 'officers-only' key-card held by the communications officer.

Nialls reached the end of it, came to his feet and shook off his fatigue like a cloak. He rapped: 'Ask the first lieutenant to come and see me. At once.' Then he scooped up the bridge microphone and punched impatiently at its button. 'Pilot?'

'Sir?'

'What's our fuel state?'

'We can make Mongada, sir. But we'll have to come down to half-speed if you want to go anywhere else.'

'That's what I thought. You'd better come and talk to me. Quick as you like. And bring your chart.'

3

The Independent Isle

'Read it,' Nialls told them, handing the signal to Beaumont.

Beaumont stood with Last at his shoulder as they read:

EXCLUSIVE TOP SECRET. RESPONSIBILITY FOR AIRCRASH CLAIMED IN NASSAU BY CARIBBEAN PEOPLE'S CRUSADERS TERRORIST ORGANISATION AS PROTEST AGAINST BRITISH EXPLOITATION IN CARIBBEAN AREA AND QUOTE INSUFFICIENT REPARATION FOR PAST INDIGNITIES UNQUOTE. IF TRUE, THIS MAY AFFECT YOUR SAFETY IN MONGADA WHICH IS KNOWN TO BE STRONGHOLD OF CRUSADERS ORGANISATION. ISLAND IS PARTICULARLY POLITICAL CONSCIOUS AT THIS TIME AS ELECTIONS DUE AT END OF THIS WEEK. PRESIDENT LOALLA'S RULING PARTY IS BEING STRONGLY CHALLENGED BY THE FREE SOCIALIST PARTY OF RAOUL MABINNI, WHOSE PLATFORM BEARS MARKED RESEMBLANCES TO EXPRESSED IDEALS OF CRUSADERS. REPORT SOONEST WHETHER CONDITION OF PATIENTS AND STATE

OF ENGINES PERMIT YOUR DIVERTING ELSE-
WHERE.

'I can answer one part of that,' Beaumont volunteered, returning the signal. 'I spoke to Dr
Almanna about ten minutes ago. He's very worried about keeping Mrs Buchan alive as far as
Mongada, and that unconscious man and the little
girl aren't improving.'

Nialls nodded. 'So Mongada it is. We'll get the
passengers ashore as soon as we arrive, fuel and
sail again on the starboard engine. All right, Pilot?'

'Yes, sir. Except if we're asked to stay to give
evidence to the inquiry.'

'That's up to M.O.D. to decide,' Nialls dipped a
cigarette to a light, 'and it's not likely now. Is there
a consulate or anything in Mongada?'

Last said: 'There's an embassy, but the ambas-
sador's resident in Kingston, Jamaica. The first secretary is the consul, and he's resident in Mongada.'

'We can get in touch with him?'

'Through the Foreign Office,' Last confirmed.
'I've got a draft signal on the bridge to pass him an
accurate arrival time and a request for ambulances.'

'Good. Add a request for fuel, and for me to call
on him as soon as we get in. I'll try to find out what's
the real situation ashore.' He glanced at Beaumont.
'I expect you're going to ask me to delay departure
until the morning and grant leave tonight?'

Beaumont smiled. 'Not in these circumstances,
sir. But it *is* a pity . . . some of the lads deserve to
get out and get drunk. Do them the world of good.'

'Yes,' Nialls agreed grimly. 'They're not going

to shake off the smell of it until they're out of the ship and into real, throbbing life. If Mongada has any such commodity.' He stood up abruptly. 'I've a mind to ignore M.O.D.'s twitching and stay in long enough to give each watch a run. We could post sentries at night and double the gangway staff by day.'

Beaumont arranged his face in mild disapproval. He was, by now, accustomed to his commanding officer's occasional irreverences towards higher authority, and at times he was glad of them, but he did consider himself Nialls' conscience in such matters. 'We'd better go if we can, sir. Extra sentries wouldn't stop the Crusaders shooting our boys ashore. And we'd have to be careful not to offend the government in power. If we placed armed men in view of the locals, it could be taken as a slight on the security of the state.'

'Stuff the state,' Nialls said. Then grinned: 'But we'd better be good, or we'll all end up supervising leaves-sweeping in some barracks. And you're right about the risk to men ashore. We don't want a repeat of that Rio affair. We'll fuel and go. And probably get well out to sea, have the starboard engine pack up too, and be towed back to Mongada.' He winked to Last. 'Then I can say "I told you so" to the first lieutenant!'

Last laughed. 'I'm all for *staying* at sea, sir. Keeps me out of trouble. And I've got so much free beer coming my way, I need never go ashore again.'

'Double or quits,' challenged Nialls.

'On what, sir?'

'The E.T.A. at Mongada.'

Last looked down at his chart. 'Ten-fifty-two local. Just as the pubs open. Done, sir. I'll even agree to paying a bonus of one can for every minute I'm late. I could end up owing you, for the first time since we left U.K.'

'I reckon, sir,' Last said, looking at the bridge clock, 'that you owe me a brewery.'

'You're not allowed to wager in the Navy, Pilot. You know that.'

'Of course, sir.'

'And I've just fined you a bottle of scotch for daring to take me to this place.' Nialls had lifted his binoculars to the sun-glasses which he was wearing against the bright glare of sun on sea. The ship was moving slowly towards a tumbledown breakwater, enclosing a ramshackle junkyard of a harbour area. Behind the harbour, on a hill that rose towards the centre of the island, a town perched precariously in sun-bleached, palm-studded disarray. 'Not the most inspiring sight I've ever seen.'

'It gets better,' Last promised, bending to take a compass bearing of a makeshift mast on the end of the breakwater, then glancing at the pelorus as he spoke into the conning microphone. 'Port five.'

Nialls regarded his navigator suspiciously. 'How do you know it gets better?'

Last grinned and waved a hand at the panorama before them. 'Couldn't get any worse.' And into the conning-mike: 'Steer one-seven-three.'

At the back of the bridge, Fiona Hunt and Bayldon stood in quiet fascination, their spirits lifted

by the casual banter of captain and navigator as
they prepared to take two thousand six hundred
tons of warship into a strange harbour. Through
the bridge windows, Fiona could make out the jetty
at which *Hero* would berth—two large green flags
were marking its extremities and in its centre, two
white ambulances sat in patient anticipation.

Abruptly, Nialls came out of his chair and
stepped to the pelorus. 'All right, Pilot, I'll take
the ship.'

'You have the ship, sir.' Last's eyes swept the
bridge instruments around him. 'Course one-seven-
three. Both engines slow ahead. Special sea-dutymen are closed up. Ship is in state three condition
zulu. Berthing starboard side to.'

'Roger,' Nialls acknowledged. And into the conning-mike: 'I have the ship, Master-at-Arms. Passing through the breakwater now.'

'Aye aye, sir.' From the wheelhouse.

Fiona Hunt turned to Wakelin, who had joined
them, and whispered: 'Why is the master-at-arms
on the wheel? Isn't he your—your equivalent of an
R.S.M.?'

Wakelin nodded. 'Sort of. He's the senior chief
petty officer in the ship. Responsible for discipline
and that kind of thing. But he doubles as the cox-
swain for special sea-dutymen. We have to have
someone extra reliable on the wheel for entering
harbour, replenishing at sea from a tanker, and the
like. In the same way that there's a special team
closed up in the engine room departments, headed
by the engineer officer. And the Navigator here, as

officer of the watch.' Then he quipped: 'The Grey Funnel Line takes good care of you.'

At once, he regretted the quip—it sounded too much like an airline jingle. But Fiona was watching Nialls.

Nialls had now left the pelorus and was making for the stairs to the starboard bridge wing, when he caught sight of Fiona. He smiled: 'Good morning, Miss Hunt. Mr Bayldon. I hope you'll have time to come and see me before you go ashore.'

He had moved down the stairs before Fiona could form a reply and she looked after him for a long moment, then asked Wakelin: 'What's he like? To work with?'

'The skipper? He's tough, fair, very professional.'

'And lonely?'

Wakelin shrugged. 'In a way, yes. He's next to God in the ship. King, judge, jury, mayor, magistrate. But he's not a loner.'

'He's very good-looking.'

'Don't fancy him at all,' Wakelin laughed. 'And *you* had better stop making remarks like that—or your fiancé will be crossing the Navy off his Christmas card list!'

But Fiona thought on, about Nialls and about the loneliness of his position.

This must be a *particularly* lonely day for him. He could not indulge his pain, his very real sorrow for the situation. Life—and the ship—had to go on, and there could be no crumbling to those doubts

and fears and self-examinations spawned by this
confrontation with death and disaster.

There must be those who wanted to cry, those
who wanted to vomit, those who wanted to flee,
those who wanted to find refuge in drink, those who
needed the comfort and reassurance of a loved one's
arms. But HMS *Hero* was a warship, and had to
retain its cohesion, its confidence, its self-belief.
And Nialls would remain the captain, the leader,
the answer to all doubts and all queries. Hard and
competent and untouched by the confusion and the
chaos, the horror and the heart-ache.

Only later, only in a moment of total privacy,
could he dwell on the day and join in his ship's company's grief. And it would hurt the more then, for
he could not share it.

She wished that she could reach out to him,
touch him, offer the warmth of understanding. But
he was not the kind of man to take an outstretched
hand.

From the balcony of his private apartments in Government House, President Joshua Loalla watched
Hero berth alongside. He was a tall, well-made
man, his grey hair still curled to the bidding of his
Negro blood, his strong face chiselled in the Euro-
pean mould that spoke of his English grandfather.
He was wearing an immaculately pressed suit of
lightweight white, and at the neck of his cream shirt
was knotted a tie presented to him by the destroyer
HMS *Decoy*. In the room behind him, in pride of
place above the splendid but never-used fireplace,
hung a picture of the Queen of England and on

the opposite wall, a painting of three Royal Naval battleships in line astern.

Loalla smiled wistfully as he looked down at the frigate in the harbour and at the white flutter on its stern. He could not make out the detail of it, but he knew that it was a white ensign. It had been a long time since *that* flag had flown in Mongada. Too long. And yet . . . the days had gone when the flag had meant protection and peace in this area.

Independence.

A blessing or a curse? He was never sure. It had been a wonderful day, that day when independence had come to the island. When the Union Jack had been hauled down for the last time. Fireworks. Dancing. Singing. All things were possible. It had given the Mongadians a new measure of self-respect, a new resolve to work for the good of their community, a new leader who had believed that Mongada's day had truly come.

But today, four years later, there was still so much to do. He could do it all, would do it all, if he were given the time. But time might end in only two days. If, at the elections on Friday, a new president emerged . . .

Raoul Mabinni. The Free Socialist Party. The Caribbean People's Crusaders. All strutting the streets like some offshoot of the Mafia. Striking quickly, silently, brutally; wherever and whenever a Loalla supporter publicised his allegiance. A bomb here, a fire there. A murder, a rape, a beating-up. Guerilla tactics. And lately, an incessant shower of circulars and posters, printed on their underground press, saying that if Mabinni was not elected, the

Crusaders would destroy the coffee and banana plantations and blow up the harbour. If they did that, the people knew, the whole island would come to a standstill. No work. No food. No future. Now, the people were asking whether it was better to have your life and a job under the Free Socialists, even if half of what you earned went to Mabinni, or be free to starve under the president?

Publicly, of course, Mabinni condemned the Crusaders. The police were helpless, the people remained terrified. And on election day, Mabinni's men would be at the polling stations to exercise further persuasion. It was a real possibility that the people would either go home without voting or —for fear of these reprisals—vote in the Mabinni regime, even although they acknowledged readily that it would mean an abandonment of the social services programme and an immediate implementation of crippling taxes.

How different it had been at the last elections! There had been a British frigate in the harbour then, too; but it had been there to ensure fair play, to keep the Mabinnis in their place, to guarantee a smooth transition from colonisation to independence.

And now . . . and now Mongada was independent and Britain could not be seen to take sides in free elections, could not prevent a likely transition from independence to disaster.

Surely, Loalla thought as he turned away from the scene below, it was a terrible thing for a president to admit—even to himself—that he looked longingly backwards, instead of to his country's future. However bleak that future might appear to be.

Nialls had his fingers on the handle of his cabin door when the voice halted him.

'Captain! I say!'

Nialls turned to face Archibald Gorme-Critchley. 'Yes, Mr. . . ?'

'Gorme-Critchley. I'm the fella who rescued the stewardess and Mrs Buchan.'

Nialls looked coolly on the perspiring, puffing Critchley. 'Indeed. I *have* heard of you—from my first lieutenant.'

'Hmm,' Critchley nodded; then added sympathetically: 'Strange fellow. Whatever,' clapping his hands, 'the press conference!'

'I beg your pardon?'

'Press conference.' Critchley leaned into Nialls' face. 'Reporters. Be here today. You'll be holding a press conference.'

'I shall,' confirmed Nialls. 'You won't be required.'

Critchley's fat face registered genuine astonishment. 'They'll want to talk to *me*, I assure you. Quite a story to tell. I . . .'

'I've no doubt of that.' Nialls' tone was icy. 'But let me make one thing clear to you. I have the greatest possibly pity for everyone who came through that air crash. It was a terrifying experience and I couldn't say how I would have reacted. I'd like to think that I might have behaved as splendidly as Mr Bayldon and Miss Hunt. On the other hand,

I might have gone to pieces—the way you did. But I wouldn't wait until I had one foot on dry land and then grab for the glory. And you're not going to, either.'

'What! I'll have you know . . .'

'*I know*, Critchley. I know it all. And if you try to build yourself to the press, and detract from the roles played by the B.F.A. staff, the press will know it all, too.'

Critchley blinked. 'I had been given to understand that Naval commanders were officers and gentlemen!'

'Never bet on it. Now get off my ship. And stay off it.'

Nialls looked across the cabin flat to where Fuller had appeared and was about to knock on the first lieutenant's door. 'Leading Regulator!'

'Sir?'

'This passenger is to go directly to the hospital to have a check-up. He's been very keen on that, I understand. Make sure that he's not deflected from his purpose.'

Fuller looked narrowly at Critchley. 'I've met the passenger, sir. This way, Mr Crutchey.'

'Critchley! *Gorme*-Critchley!'

'Gorme-less!' Fuller muttered as he laid a firm hand on Critchley's arm.

Nialls turned away to hide his smile and went into his cabin. He kept the smile to greet Fiona and Bayldon, who were seated awaiting his arrival, and waved to Bayldon not to rise.

'Sorry to keep you. But I did want to see you before the press start arriving. I have news for you, and I'd also like your agreement to hold the press conference onboard, at a time to be arranged.'

'Certainly, sir.' Bayldon was tired and drawn. 'Your news, sir?'

'Well, I'm not sure that this is common knowledge yet, but it will be shortly and you'd better be forewarned.' He paused. 'It seems likely that your aircraft was sabotaged by the Caribbean People's Crusaders terrorist movement. They're this area's equivalent of the Black September organisation and they operate on a sort of I.R.A. basis throughout these islands. We've had trouble with them in the Navy—bomb threats to ships in Caribbean ports —and they're not to be taken lightly. I wouldn't think that they'd plan to attack you now, as individuals, but do be careful while you're ashore here.'

Bayldon shook his head in obvious distress. 'What a senseless waste of life! Probably, most of our passengers had never *heard* of these Crusader people.'

'That's precisely why they do these things, Mr Bayldon. As with Northern Ireland and Munich: to draw attention to causes and supposed grievances. That's why I've been encouraged to refuel and go to sea as soon as I can—*Hero* might make a tempting target for the Crusaders.'

'You're leaving?' Fiona's blue eyes had widened. 'What about your engine trouble?'

'We can go to sea on one engine.' Nialls smiled. 'But we're not really running away, Miss Hunt. It's a case of discretion being the better part of the proverbial: there's nothing to keep us here.'

'But . . . the inquiry?' asked Bayldon.

'My writer staff are typing up statements now.
London has told us to give them to the consul.
And we'll have landed everything gained in the
search before we go, so the inquiry shouldn't be
hampered. I'm sorry to say that the *Tarrametta*
hasn't found anyone else, so . . .'

He wheeled round to the noise of the door as
Beaumont came crashing into the cabin, white-
faced and breathless.

'Critchley, sir,' he gasped. 'Sniper on the hill.
Shot him dead as he stepped off the gangway.'

4

Something Special

'Oh God!' Fiona exclaimed, and covered her face in her hands.

Bayldon, too, passed a hand over his eyes; and seemed to shrink within himself.

Nialls asked: 'Any of the ship's company hurt?'

'No, sir. There was only one shot.'

'The sniper?'

Beaumont shrugged. 'Halfway across town by now. But he might come back and I can't get everyone under cover: we've still got to ship the corpses out. And a lot of wreckage. Do I arm the gangway staff?'

'They'd shoot each other. Or else some innocent bystander.' Nialls gave himself a cigarette. 'They're all too tense, too rattled. And damned tired. All the necessary ingredients to make them trigger-happy.' He blew out smoke. 'On the other hand . . . all right, arm them with sub-machine-guns and rifles. But no ammunition. Well try to discourage snipers without risking the whole town in a shooting war.'

'Aye, aye, sir.' Beaumont made for the still-open door.

'And chase me up a taxi. I must get to see the consul.'

'Oh—consul's onboard, sir. He's in the hangar, talking to Chief about fuel. He was delayed getting here by a bomb-scare in the streets. Evidently the I.R.A. have nothing on these Crusader boys.'

Nialls nodded. 'So I've heard. But I still want to go ashore, Derek. I'll go back to the embassy with him.'

'Sir, it's . . . in the circumstances!'

'Exactly.' Nialls nodded again. 'The circumstances. Circumstances in which we're going to have sailors out in the open, carrying bodies ashore, patrolling the upper deck. They're more likely to do so willingly if the captain doesn't seem too scared to leave his cabin!'

'Yes, sir,' Beaumont acknowledged resignedly. 'Shall I report the latest situation to M.O.D.?'

'Yes. Immediate signal.'

Nialls turned back to his visitors, to find Fiona staring at him with tear-brimmed eyes.

'Poor Mr Critchley,' she said softly.

Nialls held her eyes, dwelling in them for a moment that touched oddly at his heart, then told her: 'I'd rather it was Critchley than one of my men. Or you, or Mr Bayldon.' He stood up. 'We'll give you an escort ashore and I'll leave the leading regulator at the hospital and he can bring you back for the press conference. Try to get some rest. Both of you. You deserve it.'

He left them, went out on to the upper deck through the screen door and walked deliberately down the starboard side, in full view of the town and with his stomach muscles tightening. He arrived on the flight deck to discover that Beaumont, Last, the master-at-arms and Fuller were all standing at the gangway, as deliberately exposed while they passed orders to the sailors handling the canvas-covered corpses.

Nialls noted that they were all bare-headed and swept off his own cap with a feeling of guilt: the faces of his men held still the sorrow and the pain of their mission. And even the master-at-arms was speaking in hushed tones.

Nialls glanced keenly at the master-at-arms, Harry Burnett. Burnett had been with him only a short time, and was finding it difficult to replace Frank Heron in the hearts and minds of the ship's company. Heron had been firm, fair, respected and popular with seniors and juniors alike; in fact, all that a master-at-arms should be. Burnett was learning, and trying by sheer effort to achieve what had come naturally to Heron. Nialls thought that he might be winning. Although whether Burnett would ever fulfil his ambition, to be promoted to officer, was another matter.

'Master-at-arms!'

'Sir?' Burnett came smartly to attention.

'I want Fuller to go ashore with the B.F.A. staff, wait at the hospital and bring them back for a press conference we'll be holding before we sail.'

'Aye aye, sir!' Another click of heels. Then Burnett swung round to address Fuller—and Fuller raised a hand to signify that he had overheard the Captain's order. Fuller—tough and Heron-trained —heard most things in *Hero*.

Nialls turned to Last. 'Is Dr Almanna ashore?'

'Yes, sir. He's gone to talk to the hospital doctors. The L.M.A.'s with him.' He gestured to the blanket-shrouded body at the bottom of the gangway. 'I've sent for the police. About the shooting. No sign of them yet, but I understand from the consul that a shooting's not exactly an unprecedented event here at the moment.'

'What was the consul's reaction to having a British national shot on a British warship?'

Last considered. 'Philosophical. He looks to be a tough cookie, sir. Merely pointed out the road to the police-station and carried on talking about the fuel.' Last thought of adding: 'You should get on with him, sir'; then decided that Nialls might misread the comment. Instead, he asked: 'Will you want to be piped ashore?'

'Yes, we may as well make a show of it.'

Nialls looked again at the foot of the gangway, and the huddled shape beneath the blanket, then went into the hangar where Junnion—still in overalls—was in discussion with a small, thin man in khaki bush-jacket and white slacks. Nialls saw Junnion indicate and the man turned, smiled and held out his hand.

'Commander Nialls? I'm Stan Roberts, the consul.' The grip was firm. 'I'm sorry that life's been so—exciting for you, lately.'

'Mr Roberts,' Nialls put his age in the early forties, 'thank you for coming. No problem with the fuelling?'

'Should be all right. I've alerted the supplier.'

He hesitated. 'Your first lieutenant tells me that you want to come to the embassy?'

'I want to be seen to go ashore.'

Roberts nodded. 'Yes, I understand. I have a car and we can talk on the way.'

'Are the press here yet?'

'Not yet.' Roberts glanced at his watch. 'They've chartered a 'plane from Port-au-Prince. Due in about an hour and a half. I'll get your Dr Almanna on the return, and book him right through to the States.'

'Thanks. I'd appreciate that. I was proposing to hold the press conference onboard, bring the B.F.A. staff back for it. That way, I can protect them— against over-robust questioning *and* over-eager snipers and bombers.'

'Good idea. The aircraft investigation unit should be on the 'plane, too. They can come? Fine. We'll ring the airport from the embassy. One point, though, on your coming with me, Commander: it's been getting rougher by the day in town. There's a risk in moving around, especially by car.'

'Beats walking,' Nialls returned. 'Particularly up hills.'

Raoul Mabinni hooked the long heel of one highly polished boot beneath the low balcony rail and tilted his chair back still further, but finding an immediate balance with all the grace of the athlete he was.

Tall, slender, darkly handsome and with a thin moustache above a cruel mouth, he was dressed in a heavy blue silk shirt and black flared slacks and

looked totally at ease and a rightful adornment of
this huge, white-stone mansion which served as his
party headquarters, *pied-à-terre* and spider's web
for the prettier girls of Mongada. Between his black
boots, outlined as if in the V-sight of a rifle, he could
see far below the grey shape of HMS *Hero*. He
smiled, sipped at his drink and inclined his head
to his newly returned assistant.

Virgil could not be said to have been an adornment to any place on earth: broad, swarthy and
brutish, his face was almost frightening in the car-
smash effect of its features, and his dirty yellow
sweat-shirt was overspilled with black hair from
his chest and past beers from his lips. But he was
efficient and his appearance belied a cunning which
Mabinni respected.

Mabinni asked: 'You're sure that none of our
bloodthirsty brothers is going to try for the press
this afternoon?'

'No, that's O.K.' Virgil could speak only in a
growl. 'I explained that the press are the guys who
give us the publicity. It got through, eventually.'

'I hope it did.' Mabinni lit a cigarette one-handed.
'Hell of a thing when we have to do the Crusaders' thinking for them; but if they get out of
hand now, they could blow the whole organisation.'

Virgil shrugged his massive shoulders. 'Don't
knock them, boss. That's their money you're drinking. And they've turned this island on its head for
you. And day after tomorrow, you'll become the
president.'

'Maybe,' Mabinni cautioned. 'We'll get a lot of

votes from people who're afraid to go against the Crusaders, that's true. But others will get suddenly brave inside those polling-booths. And if Loalla does make it, we may as well start looking for another racket. The Crusaders won't keep us for another four years, till the next elections.'

Virgil nodded. 'But ten to one—if Loalla does get in again—the Crusaders'll assassinate him.'

'If they do, I don't want to be within a thousand miles of this island. That's the one thing that would band these people together. A martyr. Someone to die for.' He drew on his cigarette. 'No, Virgil, we've got to win a straight election. That would put me in the right, in a defensible position. President of Mongada. Four years to rake it in.'

'You and the Crusaders.'

Mabinni laughed. 'Enough for both, if I'm clever. And I'll be clever.'

Virgil had put down his beer to scratch at his ribs. Now, he lifted his glass again and stood with a foot on the balcony, staring down at the harbour. He said: 'I forgot to tell you that they want to have a crack at that frigate.'

'Oh?' Mabinni smiled. 'What are they going to do? Sink it with rifle-fire?'

'Some of them are stupid enough to try. But it's leaving harbour tonight, anyway.'

'It had better. Because if it doesn't, it'll start to worry me. Too many of our good Mongadians remember the old days, when the Navy came in to give them heart. I want it out of the way tomorrow.'

'No, it won't bother you, boss. The English don't

want to get involved in Mongadian politics these
days. They've got their own problems.'

'In that case,' Nialls said heatedly, 'we should
bloody well *get* involved!'

'I agree.' Roberts came out of his chair to re-
plenish Nialls' drink. 'But there are only two frigates on station. You and *Phoebe*. You can't be
everywhere.'

They were in the embassy drawing-room and
Nialls had just heard the details of the Mongadian
political situation.

'The fact is,' he stressed, 'that we *are* here. By
accident or act of God or whatever. We're here,
and we could stay here. I could land as many of the
ship's company as possible tonight and tomorrow,
to show a uniformed presence in the streets, without
giving the appearance of patrolling the town. And
on Friday, an extraordinarily large number of the
ship's company would show intense curiosity about
polling stations.'

'You could lose some sailors.'

Nialls glared at him. '*Hero* is a warship, not a
pleasure cruiser. If there was nothing to choose
between Loalla and Mabinni, I wouldn't risk my
sailors' getting a cold here; but when it comes down
to freedom or tyranny . . .'

Roberts grinned. 'Now you sound like one of
my lot! But do you really think your sailors would
be content to lay down their lives for the future of a
place called Mongada; over three thousand miles
away from home and beauty?'

'I like to think that my ship's company are rather

special, Mr Roberts. In the early hours of this morning, in darkness and rough seas, they were out in small boats; risking their lives to find anonymous people. Some of those passengers were West Indians. I don't believe my sailors stopped to wonder about nationality then.'

'Yes, but . . .'

'But it's not my decision. Has Loalla asked for the assistance of the Navy to maintain law and order?'

'Not . . . officially,' Roberts countered slowly.

'What's that supposed to mean?'

Roberts paused, looking down at his glass as he swirled the ice in it. He said: 'Loalla's in a difficult position. He took the country over from Britain and as much as anything else, he has to prove that he can run it without Britain's help. If he called in the Royal Navy, officially, Mabinni would have him over a barrel, claim that he was a puppet of the British Government, that Mongada wasn't truly independent under Loalla, that Loalla was inviting occupation, that he wasn't strong enough on his own two feet to rule the country. So Loalla came and asked me if I could arrange to have a warship put in here in some supposed emergency. Ironically, he even suggested that the excellence of his hospital could have something to do with the ruse.

'Well, I thought about it for a long time. The trouble is that . . . well, one of the faults that someone in my position can develop is over-identification with the country to which one's accredited. You can suddenly see Mongada as the most important place on the planet, its problems as the most burning issues. They watch out for it at home; and if you're found guilty, you've had it. No one trusts your sense of judgement again.

'So, perhaps to my shame, I decided not to become too overtly enthusiastic for Loalla's rather odd scheme. I reported it, but in flat and antiseptic terms. And predictably, it evoked no reaction whatsoever in Whitehall.'

Roberts pulled at his drink, before continuing: 'To be fair to myself, the security situation here wasn't so bad at that time; it's deteriorated rapidly over the last couple of days. I was examining my conscience again when I got the M.O.D. request for dipclear for you to bring in the air disaster victims. It seemed like the answer to a prayer. Then, when you came up and asked to spend three days in harbour with engine trouble, it was a miracle.

'But then . . . this link between the air crash and the Crusaders, and naturally M.O.D. got worried about your being a target. And I can't argue with that. It's a pity that your engine trouble isn't enough to . . .' he shook his head. 'I'm rambling.'

'Wishing too hopefully,' Nialls amended. 'I've got to give M.O.D. the truth. If I can move, I've got to say so. There could be another aircraft go down, the *Tarrametta* could go on fire, a volcano could erupt. But I'm willing to send a joint message with you, to the Foreign Office and the M.O.D., giving the new, deteriorated situation and saying that we both believe that *Hero* should remain in Mongada until Saturday.'

'You'd risk . . . making a fool of yourself. You've been here only an hour or two, and there must be

some folk in your Ministry who regard political
assessments by serving officers as uninformed spe-
culation.'

'Undoubtedly,' Nialls nodded, 'but the Board of
Admiralty would listen. And if the Foreign Office
asked for us to stay, they'd agree.'

Roberts smiled widely. 'Well then! Let's try it!
And if they think we're both mad, and certify us,
we can always buy a farm together.'

'Or,' Nialls grinned back, 'open a holiday camp
on Mongada. Beaches, bullets and bombs. Butlins
couldn't stand *that* kind of competition!'

'Clothes, toothpaste,' the master-at-arms explained
self-consciously. 'They'll have to buy some things.
Especially the ladies.'

Beaumont looked down at the pile of money on
his desk. 'That's a lot of toothpaste, Master. How
much is there?'

Burnett consulted a piece of paper. 'One thousand and fifty-three pounds, sir. We accepted notes
only, sir.' He shuffled his feet. 'There's a card as
well, but it's just a postcard, I'm afraid. NAAFI
didn't have anything suitable.'

Beaumont glanced at the picture of Dartmoor,
then turned the card over and read in the master's
distinctive handwriting: 'To our new friends, from
the ship's company of HMS *Hero*. With best wishes
for a speedy recovery and a happy homecoming.'

Burnett scratched his ear. 'Didn't know what to
say, sir. Difficult to put anything into words.'

'I think it fits the bill admirably,' Beaumont told

him. 'And I think it's a wonderful gesture. How long did it take to collect it?'

'I didn't start it, sir. Gunners' mess came to me this morning and suggested it. We went from there.'

Beaumont lifted the money, snapped rubber bands around the bundles and handed them back to Burnett. 'I'd like you to deliver it yourself. Take it up to the hospital, to Mr Bayldon. And insist that Bayldon and the Hunt girl have a share of it. You can take a couple of hands as well, as escort for any shopping party this afternoon.'

'Aye aye, sir.' Burnett came to attention, then about-turned and left the cabin, narrowly avoiding a collision with Last, who was about to enter.

'If you're handing out bribes,' Last said cheerfully, 'don't forget the navigator. While he's still alive. And he very nearly ceased to be so a moment ago.'

Beaumont looked up at him. 'Are you trying to communicate something vital?'

'I am; two things vital. The first is that some bastard's just taken another shot at us. Missed, but scared the hell out of the navigating officer. Shot did pass between the navigating officer's legs; which could have been bad news for the navigating officer, if you think about it.'

'Did you see where it came from?'

Last smiled disparagingly. 'I didn't do much looking around for a while. Had my face shoved into the flight deck. But it was somewhere on the hill.'

Beaumont returned the smile. 'You take the near-loss of your manhood very lightly. Were the gangway staff badly shaken up?'

'Not badly. But, anyway, my second point is more serious. And I don't know what we can do about it. The fuelling company's refused to supply us. We could be stuck here as an Aunt Sally for the Crusaders.'

5

Ships will Pass

'Refused?' Beaumont's humour had gone. 'Why?'

'They *say* they're on strike. But they weren't on strike earlier today. I reckon they've been got at. By the Crusaders.'

'And you stand here and talk about minor things like being shot at, instead of reporting that we can't get underway!'

'There's nothing we can do about it,' Last protested, 'until the consul gets here. He's on his way back to the ship with the captain. I've told Chief and he's still having a fairly hectic argument with the supplier. But it's clear we ain't gettin' no fuel.'

Beaumont groped for a cigarette. 'Doesn't make sense. The Crusaders won't want us here during the last run-up to the elections. Unless . . .' his eyes narrowed '. . . unless they plan a grand slam against the ship to continue their publicity campaign. Something that's going to take time to mount. Or—Christ!' He came rapidly to his feet, scattering papers from the desk. 'And you say there's nothing we can do! You'd better stick to taking the ship round corners. You obviously can't think without the benefit of a chart!'

Last stared at him.

'Think, Bob!' implored Beaumont. 'If the Crusaders have enough influence on the fuelling company to keep them away, it could be that they're friendly. Which means that if they're planning something for *this afternoon*, they wouldn't want the fuellers on the scene and put at risk!'

Now, Last was startled. 'But what could they do?'

'I don't know. And we may not find out until it's too late! Issue ammunition to the gangway staff. And whistles and tin helmets. And post upper deck sentries. Both sides. Starboard side to cover the town, port side to cover the sea-approach. And let me know as soon as the captain gets onboard.'

'Aye aye, sir.' Last made to go.

'And, Bob. It's all very well to be cool and anchor-faced under fire, but there comes a time when it doesn't do us any harm to panic a bit. It might keep us alive!'

'All right,' Nialls said, 'you can leave them armed; but make sure that they're all properly briefed. No firing unless they have very good reason to believe that they or the ship are at direct risk. And challenge first, whenever possible. Now,' he looked past Beaumont and Last to Roberts, seated on the far side of the cabin, 'this seems a very odd situation to me. Derek may be right, and the Crusaders may be planning something. But it must be in their best interests to get rid of us.'

c

'I'd have thought so,' Roberts concurred. 'And I don't understand this strike. The fuelling company is owned by a man called Ortez. He's a minister in Loalla's cabinet and he wouldn't be easily pressurised by the Crusaders. It sounds to me like Loalla himself is behind this.'

'In which case,' Nialls countered grimly, 'I want to see Loalla. I sympathise with him, and I want to stay, but I also want my ship fuelled against any emergency. Can you get on to his office and make an urgent appointment for me? If possible, as soon as the press conference is over?'

'I'll try.' Roberts stood up. 'Have you got a line to shore?'

Last nodded. 'In the hangar. I'll show you.'

'Pilot,' Nialls checked him, 'when you've done that, get a signal off to M.O.D. about the fuel and ask about the possibility of getting a tanker diverted to us.'

'Right, sir. But I doubt if there's a tanker within two or three days' steaming of us. And we haven't fuel even to meet it halfway.'

'All the more reason for me to see Loalla.' Nialls waited until Roberts and Last had gone, then turned to Beaumont. 'Everything ready for the press?'

'Yes, sir. We've rigged the junior rates' dining-hall. And Dr Almanna's back. I'm afraid that old Mrs Buchan didn't stay the course. But the others are all thought to be out of danger now.'

'Mrs Buchan? That's going to upset Fiona Hunt. Poor kid. You've sent for her, and Bayldon?'

'They should be on their way now, with Fuller.

The master's up at the hospital, too. With over a thousand pounds in cash. Collected by the ship's company for the survivors.' Beaumont smiled. 'I thought of chipping in from wardroom funds, then decided to leave it. It was the sailors' idea.'

Nialls nodded agreement. 'And it proves something. *We* didn't think of it.'

'No, we didn't. But we might have done, eventually. What impresses me is that they thought of it so quickly. They have a knack of getting their priorities right. Makes you wonder what kind of Navy it would be, if they were any different.'

'There wouldn't *be* a Navy,' Nialls said. 'That's what I was trying to explain to Roberts at the embassy.' He told Beaumont of the agreement to send a joint signal, and to attempt to gain permission to remain in Mongada. He concluded: 'As I see it, we've a clear duty here.'

'I'd say so,' Beaumont affirmed. 'But I'd be happier if we were fuelled up. Sort of keep the backdoor open. Can I brief the officers on all this?'

'Yes, and get them to brief their divisions on the essential points. Ship's company have a right to know why they're being shot at. And while you're doing that, I'll see to the press. Dr Almanna will be there?'

'He knows. He's been with the yeoman, doing a casualty follow-on on Mrs Buchan. You going to give him a good chuck-up to the reporters?'

Nialls nodded. 'Almanna, Bayldon, Miss Hunt. It's their stage.'

An hour and twenty minutes later, Nialls was back in his cabin, having bade farewell to the airport-bound Dr Almanna. The doctor, laden with cap-tallies, ship's pictures and addresses to be looked up, if ever he came to England, had gone; almost as hurriedly as he had arrived.

Nialls had liked the man, and regretted that time had not permitted a fuller exploration of their acquaintance; but such was life. This kind of life, anyway. Ships did, indeed, pass in the night. A month from now, Fiona Hunt and . . .

He smiled at his reaction to the name. The press conference had been bruising, exhausting and depressing. He had faced the world's press before—when *Hero* had been involved in the Hafsida affair in North Africa—and he had known what to expect. Fiona Hunt had not. But she had done wonderfully well.

And rightfully, she had been the centre of press interest. Dressed in a hastily bought cotton shirt and short skirt, both in black, she had looked extraordinarily lovely; a strange compendium of delicacy and steel, fragility and strength, vivacity and sorrow. And so very young. Twenty, she had told the reporters without hesitation or affectation. Sixteen years younger than himself.

He smiled again as he decided that he might do well to remember that—and the ring on her left hand. He had never before seen her out of that loose, all-concealing red sweater; and it had come as much in shock as in thrill to realise that she had touched in him a chord from a half-forgotten song of long ago . . .

Then the train of thought was broken by a knock on the door. Nialls looked up: 'Come in, Bill.'

Bill Kiley, the weapons and electrical engineer officer, was—at forty-two—the oldest man in the ship, a lieutenant-commander and now passed over for promotion. Initially, he had been embittered at being placed under the command of a younger man, and Nialls had had trouble with him. Latterly, however, Kiley had proved himself master of his profession, and a useful member of the team.

Now, though, he was behaving in a manner reminiscent of earlier times: twisting his cap in his hands, sullen and obviously about to launch into a complaint.

'Sit down,' invited Nialls. 'I was about to ring for a cup of tea, if you'd fancy one.'

'No, thank you, sir,' Kiley took a deep breath. 'Number One's been briefing us.'

'I asked him to.'

'And you're going to try and stay here?'

'I've suggested it to the Foreign Office and the Ministry of Defence. You don't see it the same way?'

'It's your decision, sir.'

'If I walk through the screen-door and take a bullet, it'll be someone else's. So you'd better speak your mind.'

'Very well.' Kiley thought for a moment. 'I believe that we should make every effort to get fuel, and go as soon as we've got it. The situation here is much worse than we thought at first. Maybe it's our government's fault for off-loading Mongada too soon, or this fellow Loalla's for not cracking down harder. I don't know. But it isn't our fault, and we can't take Mongada back to pre-independence days. Nor can we right all the wrongs in the world. The Americans tried that, and look what happened to them in Vietnam.'

'We're a fighting service, Bill. And even in peace-time, we must accept certain causes and courses. In defence of justice.'

'In defence of our *homeland*! But this place can't be defended. The whole set-up here's unstable. Maybe we *can* win Loalla another term of office, but there'll be a next time . . . it's only a matter of luck—good or bad—that there's a British ship here now.'

'Agreed. But time is what Loalla needs. To stabilise, to build, to grow. To give a whole country a better life.'

Kiley shrugged. 'I'm sorry, sir. Maybe I'm being very selfish, but I don't think it's our fight. Mongada's not our responsibility; the ship's company is. They shouldn't be asked to face the Crusaders.'

'Say,' Nialls paused, 'that the Russians attacked America tonight. Would you agree that we should take sides in that?'

'Well, yes! We have a moral obligation by N.A.T.O.'

Nialls half-smiled. 'Exactly. But moral obligations can't be tied to pieces of paper, Bill. We're here; we've seen a wrong and we could be given the opportunity to put it right. All I've done is draw London's attention to a changed situation. The orders will come from there. And we'll obey those orders, whatever they are. All right?'

'Well, I . . .'

'Bill, it's too easy to draw a line on the map of the world, and stand one side and ignore what's happening on the other. But if you ever watched any of the Apollo moon shots and saw some of those pictures of Earth they sent back, it must have struck you that the world's really too small to denounce responsibility for any part of it. And this is a part of *our* world, Bill. Because we're *here*.'

Nialls turned to the door and Roberts' perfunctory knock.

Roberts said: 'Oh, sorry. Didn't know you were busy.'

'No, come in,' Nialls returned, masking his relief. 'Have you met Bill Kiley, our W.E.O.?'

'Yes,' Roberts smiled to Kiley, 'in the wardroom.'

Kiley stood up, hesitated and then muttered: 'If you'll excuse me, sir . . .'

He left, and Roberts smiled again: 'Not the happiest of souls.'

'He's all right,' Nialls defended loyally.

'I know,' Roberts confessed, 'that he doesn't like the idea of dying outside his front parlour. He was ranting on in the wardroom. And getting a hard time in reply from Junnion and Wakelin. I think that's what really got him.'

Nialls nodded. 'I respect his opinion, but I can't agree with it. Not in these circumstances. Any news from Loalla?'

'That's what I came in about. His office has just rung back. We're invited to dinner tonight.'

'*Dinner?* I don't want to wait until dinner. I want to be *refuelled* by dinner!'

'Commander,' Roberts adopted a resigned tone, 'you don't yet know Joshua Loalla. All Royal Naval officers are the sons of dukes and noblemen. They are above discussing commerce, but not beyond some polite after-dinner conversation. And he's also the president of this country. You don't say "no".'

'I'll have a few things to say to him when I do see him. Yes, Yeoman?'

Dancer had appeared in the doorway. He handed across a clip-board and Nialls read the signal, from Commander-in-Chief Fleet. It said:

RFA WAVE GALLANT DISPATCHED TO RENDEZ-
VOUS OFF MONGADA BUT CANNOT ARRIVE BEFORE
1100 LOCAL TIME FRIDAY. REPORT EARLIEST ANY
CHANGE IN STRIKE SITUATION.

'Thank you.' Nialls gave back the clip-board. 'Ask the first lieutenant, engineer officer and navigator to come and see me. Show them the signal.' And to Roberts: 'What time's dinner?'

'Eight for eight-fifteen. Another touching element in Loalla's character: the invitation is extended also to our ladies.'

'*What?* Does he expect me to import one by charter, or does he believe that we *do* have wives in every port?'

Roberts laughed. 'It's a ploy! If there are girls there, we can't get really tough with him until after dinner, when the ladies withdraw and the gentlemen hit the port. By which time, he's had a chance to assess you. He's a politician, remember, and a very good one. But don't worry: I'll telephone my wife and arrange a suitable partner.'

'If you would,' absently. Then, with an odd premonition and a sense of daring: 'No, don't fix me a partner. I'll ask Fiona Hunt. She's had a rough time of it and with Mrs Buchan dying today . . . do her good to dress up. I take it the shops ashore are still open?'

'Oh, yes. I'll collect her on the way home and take her round some reasonable dress-shops. Then she can come home and get ready at the embassy. My wife will help with anything she needs. Pick you up here about ten to eight?'

'Make it seven-thirty. We'll have a drink before we go.'

'Thank you.' Roberts grinned. 'But we don't need many—Loalla's generous with his booze.'

'Then let's persuade him to be as generous with his fuel,' Nialls told him.

As Roberts left, the trio of Beaumont, Junnion and Last arrived together. Nialls waved them to chairs, then said: 'I'm going to dinner with the president tonight, to try to get some fuel out of him for tomorrow. In the meantime, we stay here and the sentries remain closed up. If you want to grant leave, Number One, I'm happy to have one watch ashore. But they're to be warned of the hazards, briefed to stay out of trouble and leave is to expire at oh-one-hundred. The ship is under sailing orders. And libertymen are to go ashore—and stay

—in groups of not less than six, with at least a
leading hand or two-badgeman in every group.
Senior rates in groups of four or more.'

'Right, sir,' Beaumont nodded. 'I assume you'd
like me to remain onboard?'

'Please.' Nialls looked to Junnion. 'And I want
you, Chief, to keep at immediate notice to go to sea
on one shaft.' Then to Last: 'Tides, Pilot?'

'We're all right until oh-one-three-five, sir.' Last
was consulting a notebook. 'Then we're stuck until
oh-four-two-five. It's really a sandbar at the harbour mouth that's the problem. But anchoring
would be another problem, sir: the island's just
the top of an underwater mountain, with very steep
sides, and it's bloody deep out there.'

'I know. That's why I'm keen to remain at the
jetty if we can—plus the fact that I don't want to
give any appearance in the current situation of running away from the Crusaders.'

Junnion nodded agreement. 'I wouldn't like to
keep moving in and out, sir, when we're trying to
work on the port engine. And anyway, we'd have to
come back to fuel.'

'Exactly. But it does mean that the sentries have
to be on the ball at all times. I know that's rough,
when everyone's been up all last night, but we can
change them every two hours.'

'I'll fix that, sir,' Beaumont promised. 'About
libertymen . . . do we encourage them to go ashore,
to get away from memories of this morning and to
show a presence in the town, or do we try to discourage them in case they get shot?'

'Leave it entirely to them. They're grown men

and capable of making that decision for themselves.'

Last smiled. 'I know what the decision'll be. It would take more than a few stray bullets to keep *this* ship's company in their messes!'

'That's my reading, too,' Nialls said. 'By the way, the air accident people are going to sift our reports and let us know if they want any more information. But I think they're more interested in what Bayldon, Miss Hunt and the passengers can tell them, and in seeing the bodies and the wreckage.'

'Talking about Bayldon and Miss Hunt,' interjected Beaumont, 'I was planning to ask them to dine in the wardroom this evening, and watch a movie.'

'You can ask Bayldon,' returned Nialls, 'but Miss Hunt is coming with me to the president's dinner. I hope.' Then: 'And take that stupid grin off your face, Pilot. The invitation was for ladies, too.'

'Yes, sir.' Last kept his grin. 'Very good of you to think of her.'

'Novel thought,' Beaumont added.

'Noble, too,' supplied Junnion.

'Out!' Nialls ordered. 'Only you low bunch could misconstrue an act of kindness.'

And when they had gone, he lit a cigarette and permitted his smile to grow around it. She *was* a prize. He would grant them that. And . . .

It was an act of kindness. Wasn't it? He was sorry for her.

And excited by her. But she was too young. And she was engaged. In love. Young love.

And he was too old to behave like a midshipman in his first foreign port. Too old for the kind of loving needed by a child like Fiona Hunt. And too experienced not to know that the young could be dazzled by the uniform, unable to see the cares and wrinkles of the man who wore it.

But for all that, he could not deny his desire for her. But he could, and would, control it.

Damn it, she was almost young enough to be his daughter!

Commander Mark Nialls, Royal Navy. Sugardaddy.

He smiled again. Somehow, he couldn't see it.

6

The Referee

'Strike?' Mabinni echoed. 'What kind of strike?'

Virgil shrugged and scratched at his ribs. 'Loalla rigged it. To keep them here. And now they're giving leave. Uniformed sailors all over the town.'

'And the people? Any change of mood?'

'Loalla posters are going back up, the sailors are getting free drinks, even some old Union Jacks and white ensigns being hung in the bars.'

Mabinni tugged thoughtfully at his lower lip. 'I don't like it. If we don't nip this new-found euphoria in the bud, we'll be back to square one by Friday. I wonder . . . damn the Navy!' He came to his feet and began to pace the room as he flogged his brain. 'If there's a *last* thing I want to do it's to fight the Navy. But if we don't hit them fast—and hit *hard* —the people are going to see them as some kind of invincible protector. And that's all they need to get their courage back. What are the Crusaders planning?'

'Post snipers. The sailors' leave is up at one in the morning. Crusaders want to pick them off as they return to the ship along the jetty.'

'Bloody typical!' Mabinni growled. 'Don't they know there are armed sentries on the ship? They fire at night and there'll be flashes from their guns. The sentries will fire back. Probably one or two dead Crusaders. And that'll give the people something to think about. *Fighting back!*'

Virgil nodded. 'I told them they're not to do anything until you've approved it. But I wouldn't trust them. They're hot-headed—and half of them have been drinking all day and toasting the great victory of bringing down the airliner.'

'Oh, yes! *Great*. They couldn't blow it in mid-Atlantic. Had to come down on home ground. And as a result, we've got a Royal Navy frigate sitting in our harbour! It won't be much of a victory if it costs us the election!' He flung himself into his chair. 'What's the name of that explosives fellow?'

'Benetto?'

'That's right. Benetto. Find him and bring him here. And God help him if he isn't sober!'

Janet Roberts was dark, petite and sufficiently pregnant to strain her expensive green evening dress, but Nialls barely noticed: after the briefest of greetings, his eyes had skipped from her, past her white-dinner-jacketed husband, to the door. There was no sign of Fiona Hunt.

He felt a great wash of disappointment as he asked: 'Miss Hunt?'

'She's been kidnapped,' Roberts replied. 'She . . .'

'*Kidnapped!*'

'By your wardroom,' explained Roberts. 'She was

waylaid on the gangway. They promise to return her in ten minutes.' He laughed. 'She's made quite a hit with your young officers.'

'I'll murder them,' Nialls vowed, half-serious.

'Oh, don't do that,' pleaded Janet, with a smile. 'They're bound to be a little irreverent tonight; after all that's happened today. And she *is* very lovely. I've never seen Stan so gallant and attentive!'

A stab of jealousy. Ridiculous, but there. As was the sudden desire to find out what was happening to her in the wardroom. But a captain should not go to a wardroom without an invitation. He could announce that if the wardroom were buying drinks for one of the party, they might as well buy for the lot; he *could* take the Roberts down and say that it was a rescue operation. His officers would be delighted. But *he* would know he was scurrying after a blue-eyed child. And he steadfastly refused to do that. He had never made a fool of himself over a woman, and that was a record to preserve.

He smiled and leaned to the button by his desk. 'Let's get ourselves a drink,' he said. 'Before young Last sends up a ransom note, demanding all the liquor I possess!'

In fact, Last was on the flight deck, talking to the master-at-arms and Fuller. He told them: 'If you're not going ashore, I'd like you to split the night between you, in four-hour tricks. Do rounds of the whole ship. Then I can keep the gangway staff here and ready for emergencies.'

Burnett nodded. 'We'll stay, sir. We've both had

a turn ashore at the hospital and I'm not a drinking man, anyway.'

'Neither am I,' Fuller said, with a grin.

Last grinned back. 'I remember a certain night in Gibraltar, Leading Regulator . . .'

'Ah, very unfortunate, sir. I'd won a lot of money at the casino and I was afraid of being rolled on the way back to the ship, so I had to spend it. And I seem to recall—what little I do recall—that you weren't much help. It was you who suggested the vodka martinis.'

'No, that was Master-at-Arms Heron. I suggested the Drambuie.'

'Did you? I must have been . . . tipsy!' Fuller grinned again and turned to Burnett. 'If you ever meet Lieutenant Last ashore, Master, start running. He drinks, you know. And corrupts young men like me.'

Last saw Burnett's lips purse into disapproval: to Burnett, a leading hand should never speak that way about an officer. God, Last thought, he's so inflexible . . . about three hundred years behind the times. But Burnett would say nothing castigatory to Fuller: he needed him too much.

To turn the conversation and escape, Last said. 'I'll leave it to you to sort out which watches you do, and I'll nip along to the wardroom and invigorate myself by staring down the front of Miss Hunt's dress. Never fails. I like my pleasures simple.'

'And often,' Fuller contributed.

Last laughed; Burnett turned purple.

'Miss Hunt, sir,' announced Beaumont, and stood aside from the door.

Nialls came to his feet, automatically tugging at the jacket of his white mess-kit, and felt his heart crash against his ribs as he looked at the girl.

Her fair hair, normally pinned up to conform to airline regulations, now cascaded shimmeringly to her tanned shoulders; shoulders covered only by the thin straps of a black floor-length dress that clung to her slender figure and lifted to the swell of high breasts at a low neck-line. And Nialls knew what her attraction was.

It was the challenge. The challenge of that singular orchestration of character that had matched in her the delicate innocence of a young nun, and a body that was a pillow-fantasy. The wide, blue ingenuous eyes and the warm, passionate, generous mouth; the gentle, child-like humbleness of spirit and the proud, sense-whipping thrust of the breasts; the fragility of an unfledged, living thing, to be cradled and protected, and the vitality of a full-grown, vibrant being, with the power to destroy.

She had indeed touched a chord in him; that chord which, in youth, had sent him to sea with boyish idealism, in search of love and adventure. But the buccaneer was older now. Too old. She had arrived too late for the fulfilment of that half-forgotten dream; he had sailed his own life beyond reach of her.

She said: 'I'm sorry, Captain. I was . . . delayed.'

'By person or persons unknown,' Beaumont supplemented. 'But you may wish to know that the morale of the Wardroom has gone up one thousand per cent!'

Nialls smiled: 'Then you're forgiven, Miss Hunt.' And to the others: 'Shall we go and wait upon the president? And remember if he enquires what we would like for liqueurs, the answer is a frigate full of fuel.'

Nat Giles-Eustace lay awake in the four-poster bed in his Chelsea flat, smoking in the darkness and thinking about the late news bulletin which had carried a brief report of the shooting of Critchley and of the political situation in Mongada.

Next to him, asleep with an arm outflung across his bare chest, nestled a dark-haired, pixie-faced girl; but Nat's thoughts remained on Fiona—his intended.

He grinned to himself. She was so very beautiful; and the one possession which he lacked in his life was a truly beautiful girl. In the garages beneath the flat were an Aston-Martin and a Jaguar saloon; on a private mooring in the river, there was a new cabin-cruiser; at Heathrow, there was an HS 125 executive jet. Not bad for a man of twenty-five. But he needed still the grace and loveliness of a girl who would be the undisputed emblem of his manhood as well as his wealth. And now, Fiona wore his ring.

And he did love her, he assured himself, in his way. And he wanted her. As badly as he had wanted possession of the family advertising business. His father's fatal coronary had brought that, earlier than expected; and plotting and hard work had brought Fiona.

But this air-crash was worrying. Her telegram proclaimed her alive and well. But if she had been scarred . . . it would hurt, but he would make himself step out of her life. He had to run his private affairs as ruthlessly as his professional dealings: there was no room for sentiment; no credit in damaged goods.

Be it in business, or in beauty.

'No, ma'am,' Nialls replied to Madame Loalla, 'I went to a grammar school near London. But my first lieutenant went to Eton.' He grinned. 'I rely on him to point me in the right direction!'

Madame Loalla laughed. She was a fine-looking woman, grey-haired but with still-flawless light-brown skin and a youthful zest that was the perfect foil for her husband's olde-worlde graciousness. She said: 'You must forgive me, Commander. Joshua has brought me up to believe that Dartmouth ranks somewhere above Oxford and Cambridge, and only just beneath the House of Lords. And that entry to it can be gained only by way of Eton and Buckingham Palace!' She looked down the table to Fiona. 'And where were you educated, my dear?'

'I'm afraid,' Fiona smiled, 'that I'm another product of the grammar school. But I have a friend who went to Cheltenham Ladies' College!'

More laughter, and Nialls was delighted. Fiona had done more than hold her own in what might have been daunting circumstances for such a young girl. She had added her own grace and charm and beauty to the occasion and—although he acknowledged cheerfully that he had no claim to do so—he felt very proud of her.

But albeit that he had become more enchanted with Fiona than his earlier self-promise should have allowed, Mark Nialls had never for an instant forgotten his ship and his primary purpose for joining Loalla's table. And thus there was in him a measure of relief when the ladies finally withdrew and the gentlemen adjourned to the president's library for port.

And Nialls, who held a belief that bluntness saved time, opened the batting with: 'Mr President, when are you going to tell your man Ortez to give me some fuel?'

Loalla looked up from working on the end of his cigar. 'This is a democratic country, Commander. We uphold the right to strike.'

'Who's striking, and about what?'

'As I understand it,' Loalla got his cigar going, 'it's the usual thing. Pay, conditions.'

'President Loalla,' Roberts said gravely, 'we would be very grateful if you could intercede, use your influence to . . .'

'Come on, Stan,' Nialls interrupted irritably, 'let's dispense with the diplomatic language for once and level with each other.' He pointed his cigar at Loalla. 'You've blocked my fuel, Mr President, because it suits your book to have a British frigate in harbour. Fine. Understood. We agree your cause and we hope to remain in port until at least Friday. We have genuine engine defects as the excuse. But

I want my ship fuelled. If the Crusaders commit another sabotage and that sea out there's full of dying people, there's stuff all I can do about it with empty tanks!'

'Commander Nialls,' Loalla was smiling, 'I don't think I've ever met a Naval officer like you. It's a new—and exhilarating—experience. Now, since we're being so agreeably frank with each other, can you tell me what you mean by saying that you hope to stay in port? Haven't you been ordered out because of the Crusaders?'

'At present, yes,' Nialls nodded. And glanced at Roberts. 'But . . .'

'We can tell the President, Mark.' Roberts sipped thoughtfully at his port, then said: 'Commander Nialls and I have sent a joint communiqué to London, urging in the strongest terms that HMS *Hero* be permitted to remain until the election, in covert support of your party. As the commander says, the ship has genuine need of engine repairs.'

Loalla looked from one to the other. 'You are both extremely kind, gentlemen. How much hope is there that your superiors will accept your recommendation?'

'It's impossible to say, sir.' Roberts hesitated. 'As you know well, there are many and diverse demands on the few frigates on this station. I would not care to raise your spirits unduly, but the Ministry of Defence and the Foreign and Commonwealth Office are not normally adverse to accepting the recommendations of their representatives on the spot. We have our fingers crossed.'

'Thank you.' Loalla leaned to refill Nialls' glass,

then Roberts'. 'I am deeply touched by your efforts on my behalf.'

'And my fuel?' queried Nialls.

'Ah, the fuel,' Loalla nodded. 'As soon as I have your word, Commander, that HMS *Hero* will remain until Friday, I shall . . . apply the necessary pressure to Ortez.'

'That's blackmail!' Nialls exploded, shocking Roberts.

But Loalla merely laughed. 'I am ashamed to admit that it is, Commander. But it is also insurance and my first duty must be to the people of Mongada. And is it such a hardship to be obliged to wait here? I am told that your sailors are enjoying the town. And I shall have some boxes of local fruits delivered to the *Hero* in the morning, as a welcome and a token of my esteem for the Royal Navy.' He laughed anew. 'And I hope to give a reception for your officers. *On Friday evening.*'

'I'd rather have my fuel. Tomorrow morning.'

'But then,' Loalla kept his smile, 'you know the saying that the impossible takes a little longer.' He dug into a pocket of his waistcoat and handed to Nialls a ring with two keys. 'They fit a black Ford in the end garage down below. Please use the car as your own during your stay. I regret that I cannot offer the services of my driver, too; but you will understand that I need my driver at this time—there are many outlying villages to be visited tomorrow, before Friday's voting, and Mabinni's men have already called at most of them.'

'Of course, sir,' Nialls returned. 'You're very generous and I'll find a driver from my ship's company and make sure that the car's always parked within view of my dutymen: it would be a pity to have it bombed while it's in my care!' He paused. 'Perhaps I can help with the problem of the outlying villages. If you can grant me permission to operate my helicopter in harbour, I can have it fly all over the island and ensure that it goes low enough for the villagers to identify it as a Royal Naval aircraft.'

'Splendid!' Loalla replenished the glasses. 'That *would* be a boost to morale, especially in the villages on the far side—where the frigate can be no more than a rumour. I'll have written permission delivered to you first thing.'

'And my flight commander will take off as soon as possible thereafter. I'll also signal M.O.D. for permission to fly you in the Wasp, in case you need to call at some of the more inaccessible places.'

'No, thank you.' The president shook his head regretfully. 'Dearly as I like flying in helicopters, I dare not permit myself such a direct involvement with the Royal Navy. You must be seen as the referee, Commander, not as . . . the team coach.'

Roberts grinned. 'You've a lot to learn about the processes of politics, Mark. There's a very thin borderline between acceptability and disaster!'

The three men were laughing together as Madame Loalla entered and, as the men stood up, she apologised: 'I am sorry to intrude upon a scene of such jollity, gentlemen, but I am afraid that Mrs Roberts is not too well. There is no cause for alarm, of course; merely one of those trials which we must accept in bearing children for you.' She smiled.

'But I do feel that she would be better in her own bed and with her own medicines.'

'You must take her home at once,' Nialls told Roberts. 'I'll drive Miss Hunt back to the hospital in the president's car.'

'All right, Mark. You know the way?'

'I'll find it.' Nialls turned to Madame Loalla. 'Thank you for a most enjoyable evening. And thank you, Mr President. Were I leaving with a promise of fuel . . .'

'I *do* like a man who never gives up, Commander!' Loalla's eyes were dancing. 'Please come and see me at any time I'm here. And if there is anything you need—apart from the fuel—I hope that you will call on me to provide it.'

'I think,' Nialls said genuinely, 'that a victory on Friday would give us most pleasure, Mr President.'

'If I win, Commander, the Royal Navy will have played its part.' Loalla glanced at his wife. 'We have the greatest affection and faith for the Navy, don't we, my dear?'

'We think,' she rejoined, looking at Nialls, 'that they are simply very clever in selecting their commanding officers.'

'We've got to be clever,' Mabinni said, 'and we've got to think big. Yesterday, we were winning this election. Tonight, we're probably losing it. Because of that British ship. So—the British ship has to go.'

'It can't go far without fuel,' Virgil retorted gloomily, 'even if it wants to.'

The man Benetto nodded in sombre agreement.

He was a tall, very thin West Indian with a livid scar across one hollow cheek and an almost tangible hatred in his dark, burning eyes. A born revolutionary, he had long nurtured a loathing for all kinds of authority, and long accepted that bombs —in all forms—caused the greatest destruction. Hence, he was a dedicated collector and manufacturer of explosive devices.

Mabinni was lighting a cigarette as he countered: 'I'm not talking about it going of its own volition. As far as I'm concerned, the direction in which it goes is immaterial. As long as it gets the hell off this scene. So we think big, as I said, and think in terms of it going down.'

'*Down?*' echoed Virgil, appalled.

'Down,' Mabinni confirmed. 'We're going to sink the damned thing. Tonight.'

7

The Magic of the Sea

'But . . . *how?*' Virgil demanded. 'Earlier . . . you thought it was a joke for the Crusaders to *try*!'

'It would have been. They'd have fired fusillade after fusillade at the ship, killed a couple of sailors, killed a few of themselves—and the ship would still be there. But I'm going to do a Pearl Harbour on *Hero*.'

'Aircraft?' Benetto brightened. 'Yeah, but where . . .'

'No, you fool!' snapped Mabinni. 'I mean, hit them with their pants down. It's all a question of psychology. It's a peacetime Navy. This is a brush-fire incident for them. After all, we're just a mob of savages. We come down out of the hills, loose off a few shots at them, and retire to our caves again. We've no army, no navy, no air force. We're not on a war-footing, and ships are sunk only in war.'

A slow smile spread itself across Virgil's battered features. 'I'm beginning to see, boss. You mean that they don't expect us to—what's the word— push up the fight . . . to that sort of scale.'

'Escalate. Right. How could they? The British

Navy doesn't lose ships in peacetime. It's unheard of. And those guards are going to be looking for attacks on them, on *personnel*—not on their big, beautiful, secure frigate itself.'

Benetto stared blankly, lost. Virgil scratched at his ever-itching ribs.

'Well?' Mabinni growled.

'It's . . . a hell of a thing, boss.' Virgil shook his head. 'That sure *is* thinking big! And before we decide on how to do it, you'd better think beyond it. The Royal Navy is going to be pretty hopping mad when one of their frigates goes to the bottom. What then?'

Mabinni shrugged elegantly. 'Who cares? *I* won't have sunk it. I'm a respectable politician and the future president of Mongada. The Crusaders are the terrorists. And they're a Pan-Caribbean organisation. I can't be blamed, and Mongada can't be blamed. No one's accusing us of having brought down that airliner, are they?'

Virgil shook his head again. 'No . . . but blowing up airliners is almost an accepted practice these days. Going for a warship is . . . it's another world, boss!'

'*No,*' Mabinni denied, 'it's an extension of the same thing. And we have no choice, Virgil. Wednesday's gone, tomorrow's Thursday and then it's voting-day. And the Mongadians are out there, getting bolder than they've ever been, because of the supposed invincibility of the Royal Navy. In the time left, we *have* to blast the Navy if we're to bring the island to heel by Friday morning.'

'O.K. It scares me a bit—a lot—but if it won't

touch us, I suppose it's worth it. How do we do it?'

'First thing,' Mabinni looked across at the still-blank Benetto, 'is to get a very big limpet mine. Can do, Benetto?'

'I got one,' Benetto agreed, coming to life now that the conversation had progressed to matters close to his heart. 'Big one. How big's the frigate?'

Mabinni cocked an eye at Virgil.

'About two thousand six hundred tons,' supplied Virgil.

'Big enough,' Benetto volunteered.

Mabinni sighed. 'What is? The ship or the bomb?'

'The bomb. Big enough to blow that ship.'

'Good.' Mabinni drew on his cigarette. 'We're getting somewhere. Now, you'd better put a thirty-minute time-fuse on it. Give you a chance to get well clear.'

Benetto had gone blank once more. 'Me? Clear? Where's it going?'

Mabinni sighed again, turning to Virgil. 'Where did they rake *him* up from?' And back to Benetto: 'The idea,' very slowly, 'is to place the bomb beneath the ship's waterline. Then, when the bomb goes off, a big hole appears in the ship. The water rushes in. Faster than they can cope with it. Gurgle, gurgle. The ship sinks.'

Benetto's brow crinkled. 'Yes, but . . .'

'How do you place the bomb?' Mabinni anticipated. 'Well, unfortunately, you can't walk along the jetty with it. The sailors might get suspicious. So you enter the water from the far side of the harbour in a breathing apparatus, swim across the harbour underwater and stop swimming when you run into the ship. Then you select a point about the middle of the ship and attach your bomb to the ship's side—I believe that limpet mines have magnets? You then set the fuse, and withdraw underwater. If you've got a compass with a luminous dial, that might help, too. Provided someone teaches you to read it.'

Benetto wiped his hands on his trousers and squirmed uncomfortably.

'I can't swim,' he said unhappily.

It was Mabinni's turn to stare blankly. Then he turned savagely on Virgil: 'I'm wasting my bloody time! He's a *saboteur* for the Crusaders? What are the rest of them? Girl Guides?'

Virgil took it calmly. 'Be fair, boss. You asked for an explosives-maker, not a frogman.'

'Then get me a frogman as well!'

'I'm not sure,' Virgil knew that he risked another outburst, 'that the Crusaders have anyone trained in Mongada. There's been no call for one, until now.'

'Find one, you ape! Buy one! And quickly! I need a good, reliable swimmer who can handle a breathing-set. And I need him *now*!'

Virgil's eyes had narrowed beneath their shaggy brows and his great fists had clenched. Mabinni knew that he hated to be called ape; it was a taunt that had been with Virgil all his life.

'The only man I know,' Virgil said defiantly through his teeth, 'who fits that description is you. Want me to get your gear out?'

Mabinni came to his feet very slowly, uncoiling his whipcord length from the chair to reach full height and stand, white-lipped, over Virgil. And a flicker of raw fear touched Virgil's face. He knew Mabinni's temper, and he had seen Mabinni beat many men; but at that moment, he recalled only a beating which Mabinni had given to a woman. A former mistress. Mabinni had been a roaring, ugly animal. He had broken every finger on the woman's hands and scarred her face by trampling on her with those high-heeled boots.

Then Benetto said: 'I know a fella. Frogman.'

Mabinni wheeled on him, Virgil forgotten. 'Who? Can he be bought?'

'He's a Crusader. Well . . . wants to be. Only a boy. Seventeen. I think.'

'Go on,' Mabinni invited with icy patience, as Virgil exhaled audibly to release his pent-up tension. 'Who is the boy?'

Benetto thought for a moment. 'Name's . . . Ricardo. Worked with those mad Americans who were here last summer, looking for treasure on the Point. Him and his sister. Americans taught them all the frogman stuff. Very good. His sister's name is . . . ah . . .'

'Never mind his damned sister!' Mabinni's lighter snapped at another cigarette. 'You said he wants to be a Crusader?'

'Yeah. We've used him. Little things. Messages. He's very keen. And a very good swimmer. Strong.'

'All right, Benetto. Go with Virgil and take him to the boy. Then you go home and get that limpet mine ready. And fuse it. Virgil, you have the boy bring his gear here. If he hasn't got any, he can use mine.'

'He has his own,' Benetto interjected. 'It's red.'

Mabinni sighed anew. 'How appropriate to the revolution! Get going, both of you. The idea is to mount this attack *before* dawn!'

On the drive back to the hospital, Nialls had tried initially to avoid reference to the air crash, but soon realised that Fiona wanted to talk about it, to face it in the company of another, and overcome it.

Latterly, she had confided to him her feeling of guilt at having taken so promptly to the liferaft and in the course of this confession, Nialls learned that it had been her first flight as a qualified stewardess. His heart had gone out to her, to the quiet courage and the selflessness that so typified her thoughts and actions, and he had soothed: 'If you'd stayed in the water, you might have lost your own life. And those you did save in the raft would probably have . . .'

'Yes,' she had nodded, hunched in the passenger seat, 'those I saved were Mrs Buchan and Critchley. And they're both dead, anyway.'

Nialls had now rolled the car to a stop outside the smart, white hospital buildings. He switched off the engine, then turned to the girl and saw the tears that had spilled from the blue eyes. So young. And so beautiful. And he wanted so much to take her in his arms, to comfort her, to provide a shoulder for those tears.

But it would be unfair to her. She could not be

expected to be strong tonight. And alone, in the
car, in the darkness. Far from home, far from the
unknown fiancé whose arms she must really crave.
It was too easy to forget. Too easy to make-believe
that the world did not exist beyond the cocoon of
this car, that they were not responsible to the past
or the future, that time would stand and wait for
them.

Her lower lip was trembling, demanding to be
stilled by the touch of another mouth, a caress, a
whispered word of tenderness. And perhaps, in her
anguish, the kiss would be given gratefully, sur-
rendered to the warmth and the security and the
strength of him. But a kiss—in these circumstances
—might open the gate to a road of no return; and
she had to live with tomorrow.

And all the other tomorrows of her married days.
If she did marry: she was young enough to risk
that in guilt-stricken confession to her fiancé.

A child in a woman's body. An enchantress in
tears. A lorelei. But the grief was real. And he
could not dispatch her to her room, to her loneliness and her night-thoughts, in her current state of
mind.

'Come on,' he said, restarting the car, 'let's use
some of the president's petrol.'

'That bird,' Monty Wakelin told his tenth whisky,
'was really something.'

'Beautiful,' Beaumont agreed from behind his
third tomato juice. They were sat in a corner of the
wardroom, and Beaumont was envying Wakelin's
freedom to drink. But Beaumont had to work

opposite the captain; tonight, Wakelin was work-ing opposite only a scotch bottle.

'Beautiful?' echoed Wakelin. 'She's a bundle of feminine sex, in just the right shape. Never seen anything quite like that before.'

'Lucky old captain,' Beaumont suggested.

'*Unlucky* old captain. He's an honourable man. I'm not. Think I'll go ashore.'

'No, you won't. Not in that state. You can go to bed.'

Wakelin groaned. 'Did you have to mention that? Did *you* think she looked like Brigitte Bardot?'

'She has the same equipment, in the same places, and in roughly the same proportions.' Beaumont grinned. 'Whose comparison was that?'

'Bloody Boswall's. He got one sniff of it and was ashore like a little rabbit. Bet he's found himself some glorious millionairess.'

'In Mongada?'

'They're everywhere.' Wakelin sounded con-vinced. 'You've got to look for them, that's all.'

'You're smashed,' concluded Beaumont. 'Go to bed.'

'Oh, all right.' Wakelin climbed to his feet, found equilibrium and made for the door, mutter-ing: 'If my missus was here tonight, she'd get the best . . .'

Bob Last stood aside to let him weave his way out, then entered and jerked his head after the de-parted supply officer. 'Monty been tying one on?'

'Got a bad attack of lust. For the fair Fiona.'

'Don't blame him,' Last said, opening a can of

D

bitter lemon and putting it to his lips. 'Do *you* think she looks like Jane Fonda?'

'Whose idea was *that*?'

'Boswall's.'

Beaumont laughed. 'Boswall really is seeing things. We'll have to stop him flying that helicopter for a while. His bone-dome isn't protecting his brain.'

'He's an aviator,' Last commented. 'Not allowed to have a brain.'

'He'd sense enough to get ashore. Everything quiet up top?'

'Yep. Boys are starting to come back. Full of rum, but no bother. Briefing must have worked.'

Beaumont shrugged. 'Either that, or the knowledge that they could be shot at. Pretty sobering thought.' He looked down at his glass. 'Can't drink any more of that or I'll start looking like a tomato. No sign of the captain?'

'You're kidding!' Last returned scathingly. 'If *you* were out in the wilds of Mongada with Fiona Hunt, would you be in any rush to get back?'

Nialls had taken the coast road north out of the town and was now parked at the edge of a palm-fringed beach which, in the moonlight and from the road, was as breathtaking as a painting. The sand was even and pure white, the sea was dark and restless and muted in its roar. The breeze through the open windows was warm and off-shore; the night was starred and here, time *did* seem suspended.

'Can we walk on the beach?' Fiona asked.

'If you'd like to. But it may not do your shoes and the bottom of your dress any good.'

'I'll manage.' She got out of the car quickly, and moved down the beach, towards the sea.

Nialls watched her go, seeing the moonlight catch on the spun-gold hair and trying to hold on to reality in a totally ethereal world. Stardust and moonbeams, dinner dress and balmy breeze, tropical beach and silent night.

Bloody dangerous.

He left the car and followed her down the beach, tracking her footprints in the band of wet sand by the water's edge.

'Just started ebbing,' he told her.

She nodded. 'Do you really love the sea?'

'I suppose it has a magic,' he smiled. 'Mysterious, always on the move, moody, ever-changing. Like a beautiful woman. It's hard to get tired of watching.'

'But this morning,' she admitted, 'I hated it. And suddenly, the storms are passed and I love it again. Life's like that, isn't it?'

'Storms?'

'Things passing, disturbing us, moving on, but leaving us never quite the same again. Love and hate. Life and death. Good and bad. Have you ever tried to find a pattern in it, a reason for it all?'

'Have you?' he countered, at a loss.

'I can't. I've spent today trying; but it's too confusing.' She met his eyes. 'Should I be sad that the aircraft crashed, with such loss of life, or glad that it brought me here, to you—'

Nialls turned away from her, lit two cigarettes

and gave her one. He said slowly: 'The sea . . . can indulge its magic. It's ageless, and it's free. But you are not; on either count.'

'But there *is* a magic? A real magic, between us?' The blue eyes were searching his face. 'Can't you feel it?'

'Feel it, yes; trust in it, no. The glitter doesn't necessarily mean it's gold, Fiona. You're a beautiful girl and I'd have to be a saint not to be excited by you. As for your own reaction . . . my ship came out of the night and rescued the fair maiden. You can't respond to the ship and so you invest its glamour in me, the captain. A commander in naval uniform and a knight in shining armour. It's enough to bowl over any young girl, particularly when she's suffered as you've done. But you have a duty to the man who gave you that ring, and soon you must return to him and to the real world. And you'll have to account to yourself—if not to him—for your actions in Mongada.'

'I'm not going to marry him. I've had a chance to think today, for the first time in a long while.'

Nialls' voice hardened. 'You're in no condition to think! If I believed that you were, and that you could be held responsible for anything that happened tonight, I wouldn't stop to . . . and I'm sixteen years older than you.'

'Nothing *would* happen tonight.' She smiled gently. 'Or if it did, and it would be for the first time—believe it or not—it would be because I wanted it that way. I'm old enough to know my own feelings, and recognise the magic. And I wouldn't be hurt—Mark.'

'I think you might be, and it would be my fault if you were.' He bent, lifted a pebble and tossed it into the water. 'Tomorrow morning, you could wake up and see me for what I am: not a knight in shining armour; but a man approaching middle age, with the capacity for young love far behind him, with responsibilities and set ways and little right to dream as you can dream, at twenty. And you'd want to flee. But you'll still be here, and so will I. There'd be no way to end it, Fiona. So we mustn't start it.'

She touched her cigarette to her lips, blew smoke and said levelly: 'I'd take a chance on that. Because I'm convinced that I won't marry Nat now. And that I could live with . . . just these few days. Let them take their course. It would have to end when you sailed. At least temporarily. It would be a natural break.'

He shook his head. 'It's not that simple. There's another side to the coin—my side.' His hands went to her shoulders, warm to his touch; and his voice was strained, caught on the emotion of the struggle within himself. 'Don't you see, my Fiona? I could survive a casual affair, but I couldn't survive you. The magic would be too powerful. It would scar us. And perhaps destroy us both. You would go back to your young man in guilt that I would share. I would return to sea having left some part of me here; whatever part of a man it is that dies when he realises that he's no longer able to ignore the advance of time.'

'I'm *not* going back to Nat.'

'Write from England and tell me that. Until

then, I must accept that making love to you would be abusing my position as captain as much as if I punished one of my sailors illegally. I can't be sure that, for you, it's not the magic of the uniform, of the rescue, of the night; or some reaction from your escape.' He smiled to lighten his words. 'There must be *some* explanation for why a beautiful girl of twenty can fall for an old man like me.'

'There is. She believes she loves you.'

It touched him strangely, and he steadied himself with an effort. This was but a manifestation of her youth: the belief in love at first sight. But then, his own feelings were not far short . . .

He said: 'Then help me to be worthy of her love. Wear your ring at least until you've seen your Nat, back in England.'

She put her right hand to his, on her left shoulder, and dropped her cheek to it. 'Romeo and Juliet, Lancelot and Guinevere, your own Hero and Leander. And now, Mark and Fiona. Star-crossed lovers.' She laughed shortly, but he could feel her tears on his fingers. 'It's not a role I'd have chosen. But you're right. And the hell of it is that I love you the more for being strong.'

He had no answer to that. Instead, he asked mundanely: 'Will you come to lunch onboard tomorrow? If I send the car for you?'

Her head came up, fair hair spilled across her face and a smile lifted on her lips. 'We can still see each other?'

'That's in the rules,' he said.

'I'm glad. I have to give evidence some time tomorrow, but they must break for lunch.' The smile widened, impishly. 'Do I get a small kiss to seal the bargain?'

'No. That's *not* in the rules. At least, not at this stage. And not here. If we're going to survive for a day or two, we have to take it slow.'

'Your hand? To walk back up the beach?'

'You're rushing things,' he told her as their fingers intertwined.

8

Grandstand Seat

'Who the hell's this?' Mabinni snarled.

Virgil swallowed noisily. 'She insisted. Said her brother couldn't come if she didn't.'

Mabinni looked at the boy, Ricardo. Indeed, he seemed barely old enough to be out without his sister. Small, dark, big brown eyes, nervous shift from one foot to the other, he looked to be about twelve.

But the girl was a different proposition. She was at least twenty, long curly black hair, defiant and plain face, heavy of breast and thigh. And very angry.

'What's your name?' he asked the girl.

'Catalina.'

'Well, Catalina,' Mabinni's handsome face crinkled into a smile as he adopted a well-practised posture of manly charm, 'we have business to discuss with your brother. He's seventeen, isn't he? He's a man. And it's men's business.'

'It's Crusader business!' she spat back, unmoved by the charm. 'And he's too young for it. His head's full of fancy notions about terrorism and revolution. Huh, he can barely spell either!'

'And you?' Mabinni forced the smile to keep its place. 'Are you a Crusader?'

'No, I am not. You see, *I* have grown up!'

'Mind your tongue!' growled Virgil. 'You are talking to the next president of Mongada!'

'I know that.' She flicked a contemptuous glance at Virgil. 'And I have come to say that I do not allow my brother to dive without me.'

Mabinni stroked a thoughtful finger on his jaw-line. 'Will you dive with him? On Crusader business?'

'How much will you pay?'

Ricardo stopped shuffling. 'We'll do it for nothing,' he said, but without conviction. 'For the Crusaders.'

'We won't, Ricardo.' To Mabinni: 'Our parents are no longer young. And our father is a sick man. We need the money.'

Mabinni lowered himself gently on to the edge of a table. He had a feeling that the gods were against him. 'Don't you want to know what the job is, first?'

'I am not a fool.' She tossed her curls. 'You want swimmers. You're terrorists and there is only one ship in the harbour. You want us to attack the British warship.'

'What?' Ricardo's hand had flown to his mouth.

Mabinni's heart sank to new depths. 'You're willing to attack it, Catalina?'

'I have no love of the British Navy. When I was fifteen, I was raped by one of their drunks. I wasn't permitted to complain. The island would know. My chances of marriage would be spoiled. My chance of marriage is nothing! I want to go to America. But I must have money for my parents first. Ten thousand dollars.'

Thank God, Mabinni thought, for some drunken British sailor! And the Crusaders would pay ten thousand dollars for a sunken frigate. He said: 'Very well. Payment on result. But get one thing very clear. If anything goes wrong, you're on your own. You use that story about the rape. Personal revenge. If I'm brought into it, if I'm even vaguely associated with it, your parents will die. You understand?'

'We won't fail. Can we telephone the ship with a warning? At two minutes to go?'

'We'll do that,' Mabinni lied. He wondered if she knew that there were armed guards on the ship. He doubted it, but he was not about to tell her. 'Now, where the hell's Benetto?'

'Here,' Benetto replied from the doorway, between rasping gasps. He was dragging a heavy canvas hold-all. 'Forgot bomb was so heavy. Can't be carried by one swimmer.'

'I've got two now,' Mabinni assured him. 'And the bigger the bomb, the bigger the hole. And the bigger the bang.' He was feeling much better. 'Nice if it woke the whole town. The peasants could run down to the jetty and see their beloved Britannia slide beneath the waves!'

Nialls parked the Ford at the foot of the gangway, told the gangway staff to keep an eye on it and checked with Last that the night had been uneventful. Then he walked for'ard on the starboard side, while Last rang Beaumont to tell him of the captain's return.

And thus Nialls had barely sat at his desk and lit a cigarette before Beaumont knocked and entered.

'Hello, Derek. Pilot tells me all's well?'

'Yes, sir.' Stiffly.

'No signals?'

'None, sir. One telephone call. From Mr Roberts, to ask if you'd got back safely from the dinner. That was about an hour and a half ago.'

Nialls noted the jibe, decided to let it ride. 'Yes, I won a car from Loalla. Went for a spin. Didn't win much else from him, though. Looks like we'll be here until Friday, one way or the other. He won't play on fuel unless we're going to stay, anyway.'

'I see, sir.'

Nialls laid his cigarette carefully in an ash-tray, then looked up at his first lieutenant. 'All right, what exactly's wrong with you?'

'Nothing, sir.'

'You've just developed into a monosyllabic moron in the course of the evening?'

'Very well, sir. I was worried about you. You must be a prime assassination target for the Crusaders. I do think that you could have rung the ship from the hospital when you dropped Miss Hunt, and *before* you started driving all over the country.'

'Point taken,' nodded Nialls. 'You're right and I'm sorry. But in fact, I didn't drop Miss Hunt. She was upset by everything and I drove her around to take her mind off it.' He smiled. 'You're not

going to object to that, too, are you? I didn't seduce
her and she didn't seduce me.'

'I'm sorry, sir. It's been a long day.'

Nialls nodded again. 'It has. You go and get
turned in for the rest of the night. I'm going to put
a sweater on and I'll lie on top of my bunk. Last
knows to call me if he needs anything.'

'I'm going to do the same,' Beaumont said.
'Would you like me to draft a signal to M.O.D.?
Saying we're stuck here, come what may?'

'No, I don't think so. Nothing's really changed
and I'd rather wait to see if we get a reply to my
request to stay, in the morning. Otherwise, it could
look in London like Loalla and I are hand in glove
to get our way.'

'What's he like, sir? Loalla?'

'He's a good man, Derek. Worth fighting for.'
Beaumont hesitated. 'Bill Kiley doesn't think so.'

'I know. I've heard his point of view.'

'*My* point, sir, is that it doesn't help discipline
in the wardroom. Having a head of department
disagree with his captain.'

Nialls laughed. 'Oh, that doesn't disturb me. I
think I've disagreed on principle with every captain
I've served under. And Kiley's entitled to state
his case. We shouldn't try to suppress that freedom
with discipline or coercion or persuasion or anything. That's what Mabinni's doing ashore, and
that's what we want to fight.'

'I suppose so, sir.' Beaumont smiled. 'Good
night, sir.'

'Good night, Derek.'

Nialls lifted his cigarette again. He would soon

have to write a promotion report on Beaumont, and he was not looking forward to the task. For most of the time, Beaumont was a brilliant first lieutenant. He ran the ship well, and happily; knew his officers and men; handled sea-evolutions better than any other first lieutenant of Nialls' acquaintance; handled the ship herself with confidence. But there were moments when Beaumont fell back on the Book, on discipline or tradition, to bolster him in unusual situations. And maybe that was the difference between being a good first lieutenant and being a good commanding officer.

But maybe not. Maybe he was being unfair. Maybe he was judging Beaumont by his own standards, his own methods. And he, Nialls, was neither a conventional Naval officer nor a by-the-Book commander. But others were; and were successful.

And in some ways, Beaumont *might* have been right about Kiley. It *could* have been undermining to discipline. But it wasn't; because—in the final analysis—Kiley would be loyal, whatever his personal reservations, and because the lieutenants—like Last and Wakelin and Boswall—were too individualistic to be influenced by what the captain or Kiley or anyone else thought about something like the Mongadian situation. They would make up their own minds, argue about it and even moan about it; but they would pull together when Nialls cracked the whip. Perhaps that was what Beaumont missed: the realisation that one did not have to be robot-like to be disciplined, that one could question without being insubordinate, that the Book made few allowances for personalities.

It was a problem.

And Fiona? Unbidden thought. He slammed the door hastily on *that* problem, closing his mind to it.

But unbeknown to him, there was another problem—immediately beneath him. And as Ricardo's hand triggered the fuse mechanism, the new problem was only twenty-nine minutes and fifty-nine seconds away.

Mabinni looked at his watch, then smiled to himself. 'I think I'll stay here on the balcony,' he told Virgil, 'and watch the fireworks. Grandstand seat.'

Virgil grinned around his beer-glass. 'Should be a lot of fireworks. Ten thousand dollars' worth.'

'Yes . . . I've been thinking about that. I don't know about you, Virgil, but I couldn't get to like that Catalina girl. She's butch. And Ricardo would have wet his pants long before he got in the water. They hardly rate ten thousand, even if they manage it.'

Virgil shrugged into a scratch. 'It's not our money.'

'Not yet. But if we were to tell the Crusaders that we paid those kids in advance, on their behalf, and then they were found—still in their underwater gear—floating in the harbour . . . the money *would* be ours.'

'It would also make good and sure that the kids can't ever talk. That nothing can get back to you.'

'Oh, they won't talk.' Mabinni shook his head. 'Not at the risk of having a knife stuck in Mother and Father. They're an old-style family—see how the sister fusses over the brother. But that doesn't make them deserving of ten thousand dollars of *anyone's* money. Especially money that could come this way.'

'You want me to get down to the harbour?'

'It might be . . . prudent. You'll get a close-up view from there.' He looked down on the lights of the frigate. 'But mind your ears when the bangs begin!'

Pat Fuller came out on to the boat-deck, yawned and glanced around him, noting with satisfaction that the moonlight persisted. Made the sentries' job easier—and his mind.

He went first to the starboard side, where Able Seaman Wallace, a young Londoner of West African parentage, was keeping armed guard over the jetty.

'Hello, Sheriff,' Wallace greeted. 'Bit borin' this. Ain't seen nothin' worth shootin' at.'

Fuller smiled. 'Pity there's a moon, or you'd be our perfect secret weapon.'

'Naw, they'd just shoot at the whites of me eyes. They get lots of practice doin' that, out here!'

'Well, keep the eyes skinned, whatever else happens!'

Fuller clapped a hand on Wallace's shoulder, then moved—still laughing—to the port side. And stopped. The harbour-side sentry was nowhere to be seen.

He passed on down the side of the motor-boat, and came upon first a propped-up rifle and then a sleeping Able Seaman Regard, slouched against a

guard-rail stanchion with tin-helmeted head on
chest. Fuller grimaced, lifted the rifle and pointed
it into Regard's face and then kicked him hard on
the shin.

Regard came instantly awake, found himself staring into the business-end of a rifle and let out a
strangled sob.

'Yeah!' snarled Fuller. 'If I wasn't me,' with
more Irish than Scots logic, 'you'd be dead and
there'd be bloody Crusaders galloping all over the
ship!'

'Sorry, Sheriff. Must . . . must've dropped off.'

'*Sorry?* That's not enough! You're in the rattle,
Regard. Asleep on watch. And in a place like this!
You're supposed to be guarding that bloody harbour,' Fuller swept the rifle-barrel in a seaward
arc that narrowly missed Regard's nose, 'and for all
you know about it, they could have brought the
Ark Royal in and—Christ!'

For half a second, he froze with his eyes locked
to a moving glint of glass, a hundred yards away in
the water, and then he jerked the rifle to his shoulder, fired, adjusted his aim from the splash of the
bullet and fired again. Then he pushed the rifle at
Regard.

Regard tried to push it back. 'You've got to challenge first, Sher . . .'

'Shut up! There's a frogman in the water! Tell
the officer of the day. I'm going after that bastard.
Get some others over the side to help me, soon as
you can!'

Fuller tossed down his cap, tore off his shoes
and then ducked through the guard-rails and dived

into the water. Before he had hit the surface, Regard
was pounding to the nearest ladder, screaming and
waving his rifle. He arrived on the flight deck at the
same time as Last, jacketless and capless, skidded to
a halt beside the quartermaster and demanded:
'What's happening?'

Regard grabbed at Last's arm, pointed a shaking
finger at the expanse of the harbour and mouthed
frantic but inaudible words. Last slapped him open-
handed across the mouth, caught him by the shirt-
front and ordered: 'Out with it, Regard! Quickly!'

'Swimmer, sir,' Regard rasped. 'Swimmer in the
harbour! Sheriff fired at him! Gone after him!'

'Sound the emergency alarms!' Last raced to
the port-side rail, saw Fuller striking out strongly
and ran back to scoop up the main broadcast microphone, stopping the emergency klaxon by knock-
ing the quartermaster's thumb off its button. 'D'ye
hear there? This is an emergency. Assume stations
for Operation Awkward. Assume condition zulu.
All divers muster at the diving-store. Away a life-
boat's crew. Do not, I repeat, do *not* open fire on
personnel in the harbour. Friendly swimmer. Man
all searchlights port side. Rig the ship for immediate bottom search.'

Last threw the microphone at the quartermaster.
'Get the book out now and make the proper pipe
for Operation Awkward. That'll get them started.'
He spun round to the bosun's mate. 'Grogan, take
the captain's car and go like hell to the police-
station. Bring back as senior a man as you can find
at this time of the morning. And if they've got
divers, bring those, too.'

He whipped back to the arrival of Nialls and Beaumont, both in stocking-feet. 'We may have been mined, sir; frogmen. That's Fuller out there. Looks to be two of them. Fuller fired, and he may have got one.'

'I'll give him a hand,' Beaumont said, sprinted across the deck and dived clean over the top of the rails.

But Fuller was doing well without assistance. When he reached the swimmers, one was supporting the other. It was impossible to distinguish features beneath the rubber hoods and face-masks, but he saw that one hood had a hole at the back and he knew that in daylight, the dark stain on the surface would have been red.

The active swimmer had a knife and was clearly bent on attack, although hampered by the need to remain near-stationary if—as was apparently desired—the dead one was to be kept above water. But Fuller's first reaction was one of relief: he had seen little before he had fired; only what had looked to be the tell-tale glint of moonlight on a mask, and perhaps for only the split-second in which a diver might surface to get a bearing. Thank God, the snap judgement had been justified.

Fuller waited until the knife had reached the top of its arc, then kicked half-out of the water and chopped down at the brown wrist. The knife fell away and sank and the hand which had held it went up to, and ripped off, the face-mask.

'I surrender,' shouted the swimmer. 'Help me to get my brother to your ship.'

'God Almighty,' Fuller heaved, 'you're a bird!'

9

The Gamble

Catalina had removed her own hood in the boat and as soon as she was brought up the jumping ladder, she attempted to take the hood off her brother—who had been laid by Fuller on the deck at the entrance to the hangar.

Nialls caught her arm. 'Leave his hood,' he said gently.

'He needs help! He's my brother, my brother!'

'He's . . .' Fuller began, and checked as Nialls waved him to silence.

Nialls' voice lost its softness. 'Have you mined this ship?'

'I have nothing to say.' She tried again to go to Ricardo, but Nialls held her off.

'Then why should we help your brother?' Nialls was speaking urgently but in a deadly and controlled tone. 'You've tried to kill every man here!'

'No! We were going to 'phone with five minutes' warning. I swear it! We weren't supposed to, but we wanted to make sure. *Please* help him. He's bleeding badly!'

'Where's the mine?'

'Will you help my brother?' It was a scream.

Nialls took her shoulders. 'Your brother's dead.
I don't want to be brutal; but if you removed his
hood, you would know that. Now, where's the
mine?' His fingers dug into the soft rubber on her
shoulders. 'Where is the . . .'

'No!' Another scream. 'Let me go! Oh God,
you've killed him!'

'The men who sent you, the Crusaders, *they*
killed him. And you'll kill us all if you don't tell me
where you put the mine and how long we have to
go.'

She looked at the luminous dial on her left wrist
and her face hardened. 'You've less than fifteen
minutes. You'd better evacuate your ship. Because
I won't tell you where the bomb is!'

The bomb is, Nialls thought. And she had said
it without calculation. So only one bomb. He had
been concentrating on the girl's every word, waiting for some such confirmation, for a slip that would
win him even one point in what was essentially a
one-sided battle.

He turned to a clatter on the gangway and saw
Able Seaman Grogan leading a tall, young and
khaki-uniformed police officer at a run. Grogan
reached Nialls' side with the policeman a pace behind, and panted: 'Inspector Perdomo, sir.'

'Captain?' They shook hands briefly, while Perdomo went rapidly on: 'I can't help with divers.
I have only one trained man. He is off-duty and
lives on the other side of—Catalina!' Then Perdomo glanced down at the body on the deck. 'And

Ricardo. So now they're sending women and children to do their work!'

Nialls cut in: 'I have divers in the water. But it can be a long job to search a hull and she gives us about ten minutes.'

'So.' Perdomo swung suddenly, cracked a hand across Catalina's anguished face and caught her as she reeled. 'Speak, Catalina! I know you're not a Crusader. And I know what your parents will think of you! Look at your Ricardo! He started off throwing stones at policemen. Now he's dead! Is it worth dying for them, Catalina?'

Catalina glared at him, then spat at Nialls: 'You had better evacuate, Captain! I won't tell you!'

Beaumont, still dripping wet, was also anxious. 'Sir, there's a lot of men we could get out. Leave those necessary and . . .'

'Everyone stays!' Nialls tried to curb the desperation in his voice, and to keep his brain working.

'Captain,' Perdomo was worried, too, and sweating slightly, 'tie her to that ladder and dangle her over the side, near the water. She'll talk then. She'll . . .'

'No!' snapped Nialls and wheeled to the quartermaster. 'Pipe Junior Seaman Clifton and J.M.E.M. Shattock to the flight deck. At the rush!'

'Captain!' Perdomo had Nialls' arm. 'I know these people. They're prepared to kill, but they're not prepared to die!'

Nialls shook off the hand. 'She could save her life with one minute to go, and it wouldn't save my ship!'

'Is the ship worth it?' Beaumont demanded in

torment. 'Worth two hundred and sixty men? We could get some off . . .'

'Shut up!' And to Last: 'Is Leading Seaman Sloane in the water?'

'No, sir. I kept him back—he's in the boat.'

'Good. Get him up here!' Thank God for Last's perception: there would have been little point in having Sloane, their only clearance diver and fully-trained demolitions expert, at one end of the ship if the mine was discovered at the other. 'Number One, take her watch off.'

Aware of the battery of eyes on him, questioning, fearing, hoping, worrying, Nialls felt terribly alone and crushingly burdened. But he had to believe; in himself, and in the game he was playing.

The two juniors, Clifton and Shattock, had arrived in breathless bewilderment. The quartermaster pushed them in front of Nialls, and Nialls' heart lifted to the sight of them. He knew that they were both about seventeen, but Clifton—fairheaded, blue-eyed and baby-faced—looked to be no more than fifteen; and the tiny, dark-haired and brown-eyed Shattock appeared, if anything, to be even younger.

Nialls pulled the girl to his side as he fired questions at the two frightened boys.

'You know that there's a mine beneath this ship? Are you afraid?'

'No, sir,' they chorused.

'The truth!'

'A bit, sir,' admitted Shattock.

'Yes, sir,' said Clifton.

'Have you any sisters?'

They both stared at him.

'Have you any sisters?'

'One, sir,' from Clifton.

'Yes, sir.' Shattock's voice was high-pitched. 'Two, sir, and a brother.'

Nialls turned, pouncing on Catalina. 'Does that make you feel better? Other sisters will be mourning their brothers today. Little boys like Ricardo. You won't be killing a ship. You'll be killing children!'

Catalina was crying. 'Then get them off!' She looked fruitlessly at her bare wrist. 'How long to go?'

'Two minutes,' Nialls lied. He caught sight of Leading Seaman Sloane, tall, fully-kitted and carrying an underwater hand-torch. 'Stay here, Sloane.'

'Please!' Catalina pleaded.

Nialls glanced at the two juniors. 'Go below. Back to your mess-decks.'

They hesitated, wide-eyed.

'Move!'

'No!' wailed Catalina.

'Well?' Nialls countered. And held his breath.

Catalina turned up a crumpled, harrowed face to him. He waited, motionless and seemingly emotionless. Beaumont was also still, his fists clenched. Perdomo and Last were transfixed, sweat glistening on their foreheads.

'It's on a bump,' she whispered. 'Sort of a round thing about . . .'

'The dome!' Nialls rapped to Sloane. 'Go!'

As Sloane fled, Nialls took two paces, snatched

the main broadcast from the quartermaster and
fired into the microphone: 'This is the captain
speaking. We have located a mine on the hull and
it is now being cleared. Purely as a precaution, personnel *not* engaged on Operation Awkward are to
make an orderly, I repeat *orderly* way on to the
upper deck and to the jetty. There is no cause for
panic and there is to be no running in passages.
Move quietly and smartly. That is all.'

He handed back the microphone, touched the
shoulder of the girl—now on her knees and weeping
uncontrollably—and met Perdomo's dark eyes.

'You were wrong, Inspector,' he said quietly.
'She was prepared to die, but not prepared to kill.'

Nialls and Beaumont had moved to the port rail,
above the position of the dome, when Sloane broke
surface. Unconsciously, both men were gripping the
rail in white-knuckled tension: time was up; and
past. Either Sloane had done it, or the girl had been
wrong. But *could* he have done it, in the dark and
on a strange mine, in the few fleeting seconds available to him?

'Up here, Sloane!' yelled Beaumont.

There was an interminable moment while Sloane
fiddled with his mask. Grips on the rail tightened
even more.

'Found it!' Sloane shouted, treading water.
'Can't get it off'—Nialls' heart lurched—'but I've
made it safe. Had a pretty primitive timing device.
Changed that. I'll get another diver and free it
now!'

Nialls discovered that his mouth was dry. He licked his lips. 'You sure it's safe?'

'Yes, sir! Positive! I've given myself another forty-five minutes or so. Plenty time to clear it!'

Nialls gave a thumbs-up and turned to Beaumont. 'Let's tell the others. And get the ship's company back to bed.' He smiled. 'Thanks for going in after Fuller. And sorry I snapped at you in front of the sailors. But you were giving hope to the girl and I had to keep the pace and the screws on her.'

Beaumont nodded as they started down the port side. 'It was a hell of a gamble. To save the ship.'

'And the men, Derek. We had to go on looking for that mine. We couldn't have abandoned the operation entirely while the remotest chance of success remained. So the divers had to stay down, the boat's crew in the water, the damage control parties closed up. I wouldn't have left the ship, and neither would you or Last. I had to crack her, or lose men. *And* the ship.'

'Oh, it was brilliant,' Beaumont said genuinely, 'but it could have gone horribly wrong.'

'If my assessment of the girl had been wrong. But she spoke of the Crusaders as "they", admitted that she was going to telephone a warning contrary to orders, obviously felt deeply responsible for her brother and was desperate for me to evacuate the ship. And Perdomo spoke of her parents and their disappointment. It wasn't the picture of a killer. She wanted to give her brother's death some meaning, to destroy the ship, maybe even you and I and Fuller—the people who had killed her brother. But she couldn't destroy those kids and when we con-

fused her on the time, she'd no way to be clever
about it.'

'It sounds logical now, but at the time . . .' Beaumont shook his head. 'You took an awful responsibility for an awful lot of lives.'

Nialls looked at him keenly. 'That's my job,
Derek. God forbid that you should ever find yourself in a similar position when you're a captain, but
it could happen. Then you'll have a first lieutenant
urging what seems a sensible compromise, and it'll
be your decision to accept advice, or go for all or
nothing.'

They had reached the flight deck and Nialls saw
that there was now a police van at the gangway,
and that Ricardo's body was being loaded into the
back of it.

'The bomb's safe,' Nialls announced to the little
gathering around the girl. Then to Last: 'I want
the bottom-search completed, just in case. But you
can call the ship's company inboard and get them
turned in. Have the divers split into separate
watches when the search is over and start a random
underwater patrol at least twice each watch. Divers
in pairs and armed with knives. And keep a boat
in the water at all times, patrolling in a semi-circle
around the ship. And as soon as you get a chance,
check out the divers. I don't want anyone down
who's been ashore and is still full of rum. At least,
not for routine work. And, Pilot . . . well done.
Those seconds you saved at the beginning may
have made all the difference.'

He looked to Perdomo. 'If you'd like to take the

girl, Inspector, I'll arrange for any necessary statements to be given to you later. And thank you for your help.'

Perdomo smiled. 'I have seldom felt more useless, Captain. I'll leave an officer here to see the mine come up, and take charge of it. With my own evidence and certified statements from your men, we should have enough. I'll call on you later in the day.'

'Thank you.' Nialls watched him leave with Catalina, and his own ship's company troop onboard. They were chattering, laughing, abuzz with the excitement of the night. But Nialls felt drained and fought grimly against the trembling that was trying to loose itself in his limbs. God, he was grateful. Grateful for his luck, for the courage of Fuller and Beaumont, the coolness of Last, the sheer heroism of Sloane and the other divers. He knew Sloane hardly at all, and now he would be recommending the man for a George Medal. And yet, what could one say in cold print about any of them?

They had done their duty. An unfashionable word. A small word for so much.

He went to the main broadcast microphone, paused for an instant, then said into it: 'D'ye hear there? This is the captain speaking. I'm sorry if I've disturbed anyone clever enough to get back to sleep already, but I want you to know that we've defused the mine and although we're completing the bottom search, as an insurance, the danger is passed. I want you to know, too, that I'm very proud of you all. Good night.'

He gave the microphone to the quartermaster, smiled and said: 'Ask the leading regulator to come and see me in my cabin.'

Mabinni looked at his watch, swore and stared down at the ship. Damn the distance and the darkness!

A while back, he had thought that he had heard shots. But that meant nothing in Mongada, these days. It might even have been some idiot Crusader sniper firing at the ship's sentries. One could exercise only a limited degree of control over the lower echelons of the Crusaders—particularly if they had been at the rum.

But Ricardo and Catalina had been sober. How long did it *take* them to get across the harbour, for God's sake?

If only he could have waited; waited to import some expert frogmen from one of the bigger islands. The Crusaders would have them there . . .

But there was no time to wait. Messages would have had to be passed, flights arranged, the operation approved. While that ship sat down there, pumping confidence and courage into the voters.

No, he had been right. Strike hard and strike fast. With what was available. And the kids were supposed to be good. Benetto had said so. Benetto . . . if Benetto had cocked up the bomb . . .

Mabinni looked at his watch again, wiped damp palms on his slacks, cursed anew.

'Come on,' he muttered. 'Come on!'

Something had to be happening down there!

'Sit down, Fuller,' Nialls said, indicating an arm-chair.

'Thank you, sir.'

Nialls examined the face of the young Scotsman. He looked composed enough, but he had killed a man and Nialls wanted to be sure that Fuller did not take any form of guilt or remorse to his bunk. To make conversation, Nialls asked: 'What's happened to Regard?'

'Officer of the day's confined him to his mess, sir. Pending investigations.'

'What exactly took place on the boat deck?'

Fuller told him, ending: 'I was lucky, sir. I'm normally a rotten rifle-shot.'

'We were all lucky,' returned Nialls. 'In a way, we're lucky that Regard *was* sleep. If you hadn't had the rifle in your hands when the diver surfaced, Regard would probably have lost him.' He paused. 'Fuller, I wouldn't want you to have any feeling of guilt in this.'

'About killing the boy?' Fuller half-smiled. 'I'm all right, sir. I know that if I hadn't got him, we couldn't have got the girl and *Hero* might have been at the bottom of the harbour now, and a lot of us as well. I'm sorry that it had to be a wee lad, of course, but it's the size of the mine that mattered. No, sir, I know that it had to be done.'

'Exactly. That's what I wanted to say to you: it *had* to be done and I'm glad that there was a man of your calibre on the spot to do it. And to go in against the swimmers. That was a *very* brave thing to do.'

Fuller shook his head. 'I didn't think about it. There wasn't time.'

Nialls stood up. 'I'm sure you did think about it.' He smiled his dismissal. 'All right, Leading Regulator. Well done.'

'Good night, sir.'

'Good night.' Nialls went to the telephone, rang the flight deck and told the quartermaster: 'Send Leading Seaman Sloane to me as soon as he's finished. He can come in diving kit. And ask the officer of the day to pass the *briefest* details of the incident to the embassy and to say that there's nothing Mr Roberts can do before morning. All right?'

'Got it, sir.'

Nialls hung up, sat down and put his face in his hands, kneading his eyes and flogging his brain. He had now to send a signal to the Ministry, reporting the attack and its successful counter. Anything else?

He had instituted anti-swimmer measures and would make a show of them in daylight, to discourage another attempt. He had thanked Fuller, Last, Beaumont and the ship's company and he would see Sloane and, in the morning as convenient to their new watches, the other divers who had taken part. He had squared police and embassy, and would now inform M.O.D.—if he could stay awake long enough.

The day washed over him.

The dash to the crash position.

The rescue.

The dash to Mongada.

The horror of it all.

The wonder of Fiona.

The shooting of Critchley.

The fencing with Loalla.

The underwater attack.

Quite suddenly, he thought that he was going to be sick.

He got up, put a hand over his mouth and went into the bathroom, feeling slightly cheated.

Mabinni felt greatly cheated, and he was beside himself with rage.

'Go on!' he snarled at Virgil. 'Give me the rest of it!'

'Not much else of it. Police took Catalina away. The ship left the divers in the water and started running a boat up and down the port side. If they keep that up, we won't get another chance with frogmen.'

'We haven't *got* any more frogmen!' Mabinni stamped across the room, kicking a chair out of his path. 'So not only is that damned ship still there; but by midday, the story's going to be all round the island of how the Royal Navy foiled a Crusader assault, killed one frogman and captured the other! At this rate, they'll laugh themselves all the way to the polling-stations—and vote Loalla!'

Virgil nodded miserably. 'It's what comes of having to use peasants.'

'It's what comes of not knowing one's enemy. I was sure a frogman-attack would beat them.' Mabinni tugged at his lip. 'Well, I can't go on fighting a faceless man. I have to meet that captain. Eight o'clock in the morning, I want you shaved, in a suit and down at the . . . no, not you. You don't look like an innocent bearer of my kind regards. What's the name of that girl, the one with the big frontage, the looker? Marigold? I took her as my secretary to Nassau.'

'Mirabel Parades.'

'That's right. Mirabel. First thing in the morning, get her dressed up as a secretary again and have her deliver my card onboard to the captain, requesting an appointment for me to see him.'

'On what grounds?'

'She won't know.'

Virgil looked pained. 'I mean, what will you tell the captain?'

'Anything. I may be president on Friday evening.' He tapped his watch. 'That's *tomorrow* evening. I'm a public figure. It's a courtesy call. What does it matter so long as I get to talk with him!'

'He'll know all about *you*. He was at Loalla's for dinner, remember?'

'He'd have known about me before then; Roberts would have told him. And I don't care what he knows about me. I'm interested in what I can learn about *him*. The fact is that the strength of that ship is the strength of her captain. And I've got to meet him. *Then* I can fight him properly!'

10

Bravo Zulu

It was a morning of callers for Nialls.

First, came Inspector Perdomo to join him for pre-breakfast coffee, discuss statements and tell him that the girl Catalina had admitted her crime, but would not specify her sponsors even against a promise of clemency for co-operation.

Then, by hand of liveried messenger, came the presidential permission for helicopter operations. Nialls sent for Boswall, determined that the flight commander's run-ashore had not wreaked damage enough to preclude an early take-off, and told him to clear a flight-plan over the villages with Mongadian Air Control.

A little later, Roberts arrived; but he had learned no more about the night's events than Last's call had told him, when Wakelin knocked on the cabin door and announced that a Miss Mirabel Parades was on the flight deck, purportedly on behalf of Mr Raoul Mabinni.

Nialls shot an inquisitive glance at Roberts, who shook his head. 'Name means nothing.' And to Wakelin: 'What does she look like, Lieutenant?'

'*Good*, sir! About thirty. Spanish-looking. Blue-black hair.' He grinned. 'And a cleavage like the Grand Canyon. I was tempted to search her for concealed weapons!'

'All right, Monty,' Nialls smiled. 'I'll see her.'

And in fact, Nialls noted as Miss Parades entered the cabin, there was little chance that she *could* have concealed a weapon on her person: her grey jacket, worn without blouse beneath, was skin-tight and fashioned to her figure, and the matching skirt was positively daring in its brevity. She accepted a chair from Nialls, sat in a flash of thigh and whisper of silk and treated him to a dazzling smile.

'Captain, I have to present Mr Mabinni's card and his compliments, and request that he may be granted an early opportunity to call upon you.'

'I'm honoured,' Nialls said, his mind racing, 'but I'm aware how busy Mr Mabinni must be at this time, and I would deem it only right if I called on him instead. Perhaps you can name a convenient time?'

She hesitated. 'I—my instructions were to arrange for Mr Mabinni to call *here*.'

'And courtesy demands,' smiled Nialls, 'that I insist upon a converse arrangement.'

'Then . . . ten-thirty this morning?'

'Perfect. I shall bring Mr Roberts with me.' He stood up. 'Officer of the day!'

Wakelin appeared in a flash. 'Sir?'

'Please escort Miss Parades back to the jetty.' He bowed. 'Good day, Miss Parades.'

'Captain,' she was gnawing a full lower lip, 'I don't know if Mr Roberts . . .'

'It's quite all right,' Roberts assured her quickly, 'I shall be delighted! Goodbye, Miss Parades.'

When Wakelin had swept out the girl, Roberts commented: 'I take it that was the response you wanted?'

'Oh, yes. I want you there—if only to stop me from punching Mabinni on the nose.'

Roberts laughed. 'Why won't you see him on-board?'

'Firstly, on principle: if Mabinni wants to come to me, I'd rather go to him. Then, if he did come onboard, we'd have to receive him with a certain amount of ceremony and that would make it easier for him to con his way onboard a second time—the gangway staff are less likely to kick his teeth in if they know he's someone important. And finally, anything he finds out about the lay-out of the interior of the ship could be of use to him, so I'd rather he didn't see it first-hand.'

'Good thinking!' Roberts admitted. 'And quick thinking. I wouldn't like to play poker with you!'

Nialls grinned. 'You'd beat me this morning. I'm so tired I have to wind my brain up every so often. Now, before Miss Parades breasted her way in, we were discussing the nocturnal frolics. Have you reported to London?'

'Only that there was an unsuccessful attempt to mine HMS *Hero* during the night, and that full details would be passed by the ship to the Ministry of Defence. I hope you've done so!'

'Yes; you can read the signal. It'll give you the whole story. I'm glad you didn't say anything else —trouble is that our latest signals would have hit their desks just as they were making up their minds whether or not we should stay.'

'So? You can't go without fuel.'

'True,' Nialls agreed, 'but I feel obliged to keep after Loalla on the fuel and I'm terrified that I'll get it at the same time as I get orders to move out. And I don't want to run away now. Not when the Crusaders have really declared war on *us*. I want to stay and watch them lose the election.'

Roberts grinned. 'You're beginning to identify with your surroundings, you know! That's a Foreign Office disease!'

'I'm getting involved, all right!' Nialls laughed. 'I've got the most complicated watch-system ever known. I've got the stokers in watches, repairing the engine; the normal gangway watches; armed sentry watches; the Awkward watches, like boat's crew and divers; and I've got the off-duty part of watch going ashore in waves throughout the day to smile at the locals.'

'I noticed that. Saw some uniforms in the streets as I came down this morning.'

Nialls nodded. 'The boys have never had it so good. Leave for some from eight o'clock. Briefed to walk around in the sun and keep their eyes open. And any of Mabinni's lot who start throwing bricks through shop windows or thumping locals will be marched off very promptly to the police-station. Very public-spirited, my ship's company!'

'Mabinni's going to get very mad. Grapevine is that he and his louts will be out and about this afternoon; what they call "campaigning".' He frowned. 'Have you told M.O.D. what you're doing?'

'I put it in terms of "intend", arguing that it was in our interests to try to keep the temperature ashore down, while we're stuck here.'

'I hope they—here's the yeoman.'

Dancer was trying to contain a smile. 'I think this is the signal you've been waiting for, sir. It acknowledges yesterday's long signal and the one you sent this morning.'

Nialls took the clip-board and read out the message. It said:

APPROVED TO REMAIN MONGADA UNTIL SATUR-DAY FORENOON. YOU SHOULD NONETHELESS MAKE BEST ENDEAVOURS FUEL EARLIEST TO GIVE MOBILITY IN CASE OF CRISIS AND YOU SHOULD NOT THEREAFTER HESITATE TO LEAVE IF SHIP ENDANGERED AGAIN. YOUR POLICY RE LEAVE AND UNIFORMED PRESENCE ASHORE AP-PROVED PROVIDED THAT THERE IS NO OVERT EXPRESSION OF SYMPATHY WITH EITHER POLI-TICAL PARTY.

2. FULL AWKWARD PROCEDURES ARE TO REMAIN IN FORCE EVEN AFTER ELECTIONS.

3. ON DEPARTURE MONGADA PROCEED AT ECO-NOMICAL SPEED TO KINGSTON. REPORT ESTI-MATED TIME OF ARRIVAL.

4. BRAVO ZULU.

'Yippee,' observed Roberts. 'What does "bravo zulu" mean?'

'It's signal code for "well done".' Nialls smiled. 'Yeoman, tell the officer of the day I'd like to see all heads of department and the navigating officer in five minutes' time. If the navigating officer's turned in, I'll see him later.'

'Aye aye, sir. I know the first lieutenant's on the flight deck, dealing with a couple of reporters.'

Nialls nodded. 'Right, when he's finished.' And to Roberts, as Dancer left: 'Forgot to tell you that we did a prepared statement for the press. With so many of them about, they were bound to get early word on the attack.'

'You didn't mention the Crusaders by name?'

'Oh, no. A very flat statement. The ship was subjected to an underwater attack by two terrorists. They were detected immediately; one was killed, one was captured. Their explosive device was rendered harmless. Even more stringent security measures have been adopted to counter any possible repetition.'

'Lovely!' Roberts enthused. 'That'll make the Crusaders look like a bunch of dummies, and it'll reassure the mums and dads at home that the boys are safe.' He stood up. 'Right, while you're briefing your men, I'll go up to Loalla's offices and demand the fuel. Meet you back here about ten-fifteen and drive you to Mabinni's.'

'Fine. Oh—I forgot to ask if Janet was better this morning.'

'Fully recovered, thanks.' He grinned from the door. 'I forgot to ask how Fiona was last night!'

Nialls looked through him.

'Yes,' Roberts said, reddening. 'See you later.'

'I don't mind if he wants to come here,' Mabinni told the girl. 'Pity that Roberts'll be with him, though. I've got to get the conversation off a polite diplomatic level . . .' He glanced at Virgil. 'We'll have you in a suit before they arrive.'

Virgil looked horrified.

'A suit,' Mabinni repeated firmly. 'You can sit in, and watch the captain for reactions, mannerisms, anything that could indicate a weakness. You, Mirabel, do the door-opening and get the coffee.'

She pouted. 'I have a job to go to.'

'You stay here and brighten the captain's day.'

'You'll be surprised,' she predicted, 'at how young he is.'

'It's a young man's world,' commented Mabinni, 'if only Loalla would believe it.' Then he paused, looked sharply at the girl. 'The truth, Mirabel. Did the captain show any particular interest in you?'

'No . . .' regretfully, 'but the duty officer did!'

'Did he? You sure?'

She laughed, and put her fingers to the valley between her breasts. 'If you look down here, you'll probably find his eyes!'

Mabinni tugged characteristically at his lower lip. 'Now listen, Mirabel. Tell me everything that happened onboard. Every detail, from the moment you walked up the gangway.'

Nialls' next caller was another messenger from the president's office, this time to deliver a note about the attack on the ship. It was obviously a note for public consumption, being copied to the press, and was full of sweeping phrases such as 'this outrage perpetrated by enemies of Mongada on our honoured guests.'

But a less formal note came back from Loalla
with Roberts; written in a bold, beautifully-
moulded hand, it said:

'*My dear Commander,*
       Delighted you gave Crusaders such a re-
sounding thrashing last night. More delighted that
you have permission to stay. Your fuel will arrive
forthwith.
       Congratulations and best wishes.

                                          Loalla.'

Roberts grinned. 'The old boy really is over the
moon. And the Crusaders are getting desperate:
they burned down a whole village last night. The
village-council had defied a ban on Loalla posters.
The headman was at the President's offices when I
got there—asking for another set of posters to stick
up on the ruins. And he asked me if you could spare
some sailors to help with the rebuilding.'

'I'm getting a bit short of available sailors,' said
Nialls. 'They can't be everywhere.'

'No, but remember that the rebuilding idea is
just an excuse—they really want a couple of your
boys there to give a shot in the arm to the villagers.
You can have no idea what a difference a Naval
uniform is making to these people. Two days ago,
they were down and out. Now they're fighting back.
They *believe* in the Navy, Mark.'

'All right,' Nialls nodded resignedly, 'we'll find
a couple from somewhere. I'm going to end up
dressing the Chinese laundrymen as leading seamen!'

Doc Peters was walking back through the town from the hospital. The sun was shining, his former patients were improving and he had had the pleasure of escorting Miss Hunt on an early shopping trip for dresses. He had been pleased by the way in which she had sought his opinion on style and colour, and quite jubilant that they should have run into a number of the ship's company on the way back. Green, they had been. Tongues hanging out.

It was a good day.

He turned a corner and came upon a small market shop, boasting a huge picture of President Loalla in the middle of its window. In front of it, an old man was working; carrying foodstuffs from a barrow in the street, into the shop. The old man caught sight of him, straightened and came up into a salute—an Army salute, but that did not matter —and smiled: 'Good morning, sir.'

'Good morning,' Doc replied, solemnly returning the salute. 'It's a lovely . . .'

There was a screech of brakes behind him and a battered black car slithered to a halt hard-by the barrow. Two young men got out, both locals, and as one hurled a brick at the president's picture, smashing the window, the other pushed the old man out of the way and overturned the barrow. Then they rushed back to their car—and checked into narrow-eyed menace.

Doc was standing by the driver's door, tossing the car-keys in his hand. He was not at all sure what he would do next, and was even less sure a moment later: both men had drawn knives.

Then the clatter of running feet and suddenly, there were familiar faces all around him. Tolliday, Blackman, Cutler, Barnes, Loftus . . . the stokers' mess to the rescue!

One of the men waved his knife. 'Stand out of the way!'

'Poke it,' countered Cutler; and if his somewhat terse message was beyond the comprehension of his adversaries, his actions were clearly well understood: he had found a brick in the front of the car and had raised it above his head.

'Don't hit him with that,' Doc warned. 'You'll kill him!'

But the man had already arrived at the same diagnosis. He threw down the knife and raised his hands.

Cutler looked disappointed, and reluctant to abandon the brick. And then he saw the two policemen, approaching at the double. He lowered the brick and smiled at Doc.

'Bloody good run-ashore this,' he said.

'Commander Nialls,' Mirabel announced, 'and Mr Roberts.'

Mabinni went forward quickly, hand outstretched and smile wide on his freshly groomed face. He was wearing a dark-grey suit, with a black knitted tie and a heavy silk white shirt, and looked cool and competent.

'Commander, how nice to meet you. And Mr Roberts.' The voice was warm, genuine. 'I'm Raoul Mabinni and Virgil,' indicating, 'is my campaign manager. Won't you sit down? Coffee? For four, please, Mirabel.'

Virgil glowered at his master. Mabinni knew that he hated coffee—Virgil drank beer even at breakfast. And anyway, drinking was impossible: his blue suit was too tight and the collar and tie were choking him. He hoped that the meeting would not be a long one.

Nialls and Roberts had taken chairs, and Mabinni returned to his seat as he said: 'I must say at once how distressed I was to hear about the trouble you had in the night, Commander.'

Nialls smiled back. 'Oh, it was a good exercise for us, Mr Mabinni. Except that they were a couple of amateurs—our new listening device picked them up as soon as they entered the water.'

'Oh?' Mabinni's smile slipped. 'I hear you're also having bother with fuelling. Some silly strike?'

'No.' Nialls was amused. 'Matter of fact, the ship's being fuelled now.'

Mabinni's smile lifted again. 'So we'll be saying goodbye to you shortly?'

'Not before the weekend—unless your first duty as new president would be to revoke our diplomatic clearance?'

'Never!' Mabinni struggled. 'I'm a great admirer of the Royal Navy. It's nice to see your sailors in the town . . . you're granting a special kind of leave?'

'I'm getting as many ashore as possible,' nodded Nialls. 'They had an unpleasant time with that air crash. Engine defects can be a blessing, on occasions.'

'I'm sure.' Mabinni looked gratefully to the door as Mirabel interrupted with a tray of coffee and biscuits. 'Ah, pause for refreshment!'

Mirabel distributed the cups, bending low directly in front of Nialls and enabling him to see to her waistline. He thought immediately of Fiona, and turned the thought aside: Mabinni needed total concentration.

And, in fact, Mabinni took Mirabel's exit as his cue to change tacks. All at once, his smile had gone, the façade of charm had fallen away and his voice was hard.

'All right, Nialls, let's clear the decks, to use an expression you'll understand! I don't like the way you're trying to influence this election!'

'Mr Mabinni!' Roberts was on his feet.

'Shut up, Roberts!' Mabinni rapped.

Roberts stood his ground. 'Commander, I think we should leave.'

Mabinni looked contemptuous. 'Why don't you go out on the balcony and sing a few bars of *God Save the Queen*?'

'Commander . . .' Roberts repeated formally.

'Sorry, Stan,' Nialls said quietly, 'I know you're right, but I have a thing or two to say to Mr Mabinni as well. The first, Mabinni, is that I don't like the way *you* are trying to influence this election. You've brought a bunch of hoodlums to a small island and used guerilla tactics to intimidate the population. I've brought in a ship and neutralised that, leaving a straight fight between President Loalla and you. And you know damned well that in those circumstances, you're going to lose. So now you're beginning to panic. Last night was the grand slam, and it failed. And the next thing you try will be even more stupid than the last. So I'll warn you: harm any one of my ship's company and I'll turn the rest loose with orders to find you and bring the pieces back to me!'

Roberts stared, aghast.

Virgil was open-mouthed, his discomfort forgotten.

Mabinni smiled thinly. 'Brave words, Commander. But your hands are tied, as your stuff-shirted friend over there will remind you. You can't break the law, and I don't have to: the Crusaders have no link with the Free Socialist Party. So I'll warn *you*—in an amicable sort of way. From what I know of these Crusaders, you could lose a lot of men before I lose the election.'

'You've lost the election, Mabinni. Why don't you clear out and go back to stealing handbags from old ladies, or whatever you did before the Crusaders made a politician out of you?'

'I'll give you a final chance, Nialls. Sail today or restrict leave. Or take the consequences.'

Nialls got to his feet and made for the door, a white-faced Roberts at his heels. He opened the door, then turned in the doorway and said evenly: 'Please don't trouble to return my call, Mr Mabinni. You'll be too busy packing.'

And in the car, Roberts admitted: 'I rather enjoyed that, secretly; after the initial shock. But you realise that he was trying to needle you, to get a reaction?'

'Sure. And I wanted to leave him in no doubt that

I won't be deflected or frightened. Otherwise, he'd try a succession of minor nuisances to wear me down.' Nialls lit a cigarette. 'Deep at heart, he must know he's fighting a lost cause.'

Roberts shrugged. 'Maybe. You managed to change the will of the people in twenty-four hours, and he's betting on changing it back in the same time—if he can keep you quiet. And he knows that if he gives up before the polls open tomorrow morning, the Crusaders might kill him. He has to keep going for another day, or answer to them. And in that light, he has little to lose in having another go at the ship.'

'Except a few Crusaders,' Nialls agreed grimly. 'Because we're ready for them.'

'I almost wish now,' Mabinni concluded hollowly, 'that I *hadn't* met him.'

Virgil was pulling off his tie. 'One thing's clear, Boss. You can shoot half his crew and he still won't sail today.'

'Right.' Mabinni got up, changed his mind and slumped down again. 'Christ, Virgil, I can't help feeling we're in the middle of a nightmare! On Tuesday, I'd never heard of HMS *Hero*. And that captain! He's more like a sergeant in their para-troopers!'

'What are you going to do?'

'I could jump off the balcony.' Mabinni sighed. 'I've got to find a way of *forcing* him to restrict leave, to withdraw the sailors off the streets. If I could manage that, and get a clear field from start of voting tomorrow, we could still do it.'

'Or,' Virgil growled, 'if the ship sprouted wings and flew away.'

Mabinni's fist crashed on to the table, scattering the coffee cups. 'Damn you, Virgil! I'm serious! I haven't finished with that captain yet. In fact, I haven't even *started*!'

11

Rally and Riot

Fiona had been depressed when she arrived for lunch, having spent the latter part of the forenoon giving evidence to the Air Accident Board; but Nialls was lifted nonetheless by the sight of her. She was wearing a light-blue cotton frock, with the golden hair tied back in a matching ribbon, and she looked cool and fresh and infinitely desirable.

Over lunch, they fenced and probed and shied away from stated recollection of the night before, and they talked about the Operation Awkward (of which Fiona had learned from Doc Peters), and the Loallas, and the price of clothes. But finally, Nialls had to say: 'We've had permission from London to stay until Saturday.'

'Two nights,' she calculated.

'Two evenings,' amended Nialls.

'Sorry,' she smiled, 'forgot the rules. By the way: they offered to fly me out tomorrow. I refused to go before you leave.'

'I'm glad,' he told her. 'And,' looking into that beautiful face, 'a little . . . afraid, too. I had wondered if it was *just* the magic of the moonlight and the sea, but it's as much a struggle in the day-time.'

'It's worse for me, Captain, sir. You've got a ship to run. But I can spend hours sitting in my room and dreaming. Such shocking dreams—definitely not in the rules!'

'How secure is that room in the hospital?'

'Well,' she grinned, impish humour bubbling into the blue eyes, 'we wouldn't be disturbed!' Then, seeing the anxiety in his face: 'The Crusaders?'

He nodded. 'Mabinni has to get at me somehow. If he guessed that . . . at our relationship, he'd make a try for you. To ransom you on a guarantee of my taking the ship's company out of circulation.'

'He can't know.'

'Not yet. But if I take you to dinner for the next two evenings, and if . . . our feelings are as plain to see as I think they must be, he'd have to be a complete fool to miss it. And he isn't that.' He half-smiled. 'I'll ask the Roberts to put you up at the embassy. It may not be absolutely Crusader-proof, but at least it's less open and public than the hospital.'

'And,' she added mischievously, 'it helps you to keep to the rules: you could escort me to my bedroom door in the hospital, but not at the embassy. Coward!'

Nialls laughed. 'You *enjoy* my suffering, don't you?'

She laughed back. 'I have to get *some* kick out of our relationship!' And softly: 'Mark, what *would* you do if Mabinni tried to ransom me?'

'Don't you know?'

'Nothing?'

'Exactly.' He met her eyes. 'I'd go out of my mind, maybe; but I couldn't surrender the island to terrorism—not even for you.'

'I'd surrender the world, for you.'

For a moment, resentment flared in him at her comment; and then he remembered that she was young enough to believe it. He said carefully: 'I'm a commanding officer before I'm a private individual, Fiona. I have to be. If I'm not prepared to accept that, I shouldn't be in this cabin. It's the price of the job.'

'You're very honest.'

'That's in the rules, too.' He looked at his watch. 'Do you have to give evidence this afternoon?'

'No, they've finished with me. For the present.'

'Well, what would you like to do? You can stay here if you want, and plunder my library, or I can give you the car and an escort—if I've any sailors left—and you can go round the island.'

'You couldn't come with me? What are you going to do?'

He pointed to the door of his sleeping cabin. 'Crawl in there and die, as soon as I've had a word with Derek Beaumont.' He smiled. 'I may have thought quite a lot about bed since I met you, Miss Hunt, but I haven't seen much of it!'

'And you must keep up your strength,' she nodded solemnly. 'I'll stay here then, if you don't mind. And read back-numbers of *Playboy*, or whatever Naval captains put under their pillows.'

'*The Manual of Seamanship*,' he said. 'And sometimes the *Channel Pilot*.'

'That sounds kinky enough,' she agreed.

The car moved slowly through the streets, guided by a worried Virgil.

In the back seat, Mabinni tugged at his lip and swore under his breath. 'Just look at them! Everywhere! Uniforms, uniforms and more damned uniforms!'

'Maybe,' Virgil offered tentatively, 'we should cancel the rally?'

'We can't! Damn it, Virgil, I'm still trying to win! And the Crusaders *will* be there?'

'In the crowd, as always. But if there are sailors there, too . . .'

'We must have *some* supporters—among the ordinary people?'

Virgil gazed steadfastly through the windscreen. He had no desire to risk his master's wrath in responding to *that* query.

Nialls knocked on Beaumont's door, pushed aside the curtain and looked in. Beaumont was stretched out on his bunk, but swung to his feet as he opened his eyes and saw the captain.

'Sorry, sir; just recharging the batteries.'

'Stay there,' Nialls told him. 'I'm going to get turned in as well. Came to ask if you want to go ashore tonight?'

'Not if you want to go, sir. I've plenty to do. The Mabinni rally's meant a reshuffle of watches: I've sent the heavy gang ashore to keep an eye on it. And I've still to work out the polling-station patrols for tomorrow morning.'

'Did you fix anyone to go up to that village?'

'Yes.' Beaumont smiled sheepishly. 'Bill Kiley volunteered to take a couple of his lads.'

'Did he?' Nialls could have said 'now, perhaps you understand'; instead, he commented: 'Good of him to go. Well, I won't disturb you—and if it's all right with you, I'll go ashore about eight.'

'Dinner party?'

'Not really. But Fiona Hunt laughs at my jokes —and as your rotten wardroom never does, it's too good an opportunity to miss!'

Beaumont frowned. Then said only: 'She's a pretty girl.'

'She is. Good night. Or rather, good afternoon!'

Beaumont stared at the curtain as it fell back into place. Then he shook his head and dropped on to the bunk.

Mabinni's rally was in the town's football ground; an arena of somewhat smaller proportions than the average English village pitch, and with as few facilities. His men had erected a dais in the pitch's centre-circle and, with scant regard for the future use of the playing area, had planted Mabinni banners around the rest of it.

At Mabinni's previous rally, on the day after they had burned down the original Loalla election headquarters and killed the two Loalla canvassers within, the Crusaders had shepherded people from the streets to attend and—with some persuasion— to cheer the arrival of their leader. But on this occasion, the ground was well filled without their aid: and the people had come prepared to barrack and to boo.

It was Mabinni's first experience of the true ugliness of the crowd and although fear never touched his handsome features, he could sense the raw hostility in their mood and see the hate upon their faces.

At first, the Crusaders—wearing their Free Socialist Party armbands—had some success in intimidating the opposition by moving among the crowd and pointedly noting names or other details of barrackers in small, red-covered notebooks issued to them by Virgil. But the noisy nucleus of diehard Loalla supporters maintained its challenge, regardless, and gradually the rest of the gathering caught this enthusiasm and took still more courage from the quiet attendance of the uniformed sailors, under Boswall and Burnett, on the periphery of the meeting. The heckling swelled to counter Mabinni's speech and the three police officers detailed to patrol the proceedings eased their truncheons and waited for trouble.

'Loalla,' Mabinni thundered into the microphone, 'claims that he is good enough to carry Mongada into a new era of successful independence, that he has pride in his country. But where's the pride, and where's the independence, when the very symbol of imperialism and exploitation is in our harbour and in our streets? Have we progressed at all since sixteen-thirty-two when the British Navy first came here to inflict its will upon Mongadians? And have you asked yourselves why the

British Navy should be here again, *at this particular time?*'

'To shoot your divers!' yelled back a tall, gangling youth with a Loalla button on his shirt.

The crowd laughed, clapped and cheered their spokesman and anger boiled into Mabinni's dark eyes as he tried grimly to resume his address.

But the trouble for which the police had waited, was at hand. It stemmed directly from the frustration of the Crusaders at their inability to quell this pride in the people and at their unfamiliarity with the task. And one Crusader found it too much that the taunting young Loalla man could not be silenced by hissed threats. A knife was drawn, a scream topped even the shouting of the crowd and the young man fell to the ground with a stab wound in his side.

In a moment, hands were reaching for the Crusader, all anxious for a piece of him. Police whistles shrilled and truncheons came down as the officers attempted to carve a way to the melee. But the crowd shut them out; passively, but effectively. And then the master-at-arms, with Grogan and Wallace, moved in at a run; the crowd, perhaps reluctant to show even the slightest opposition to their allies, parted as a bow-wave and the Crusader was plucked away from them and delivered to the grateful police.

And in the next moment, as if at a signal, a barrage of sticks and stones and fruit filled the sky and rained down in anger on the dais. The Crusaders fell back around their leader as the crowd surged forward, and it was no longer a meeting but

a potential battleground. Knives flashed in the sun,
faces contorted in fear and fury and the three
policemen gathered themselves for a brave but des-
pairing effort to restore order.

Boswall's orders rang out through his cupped
hands as the sailors ran to group around him.

'Master, get a double line of men in there, all
the way through to the stage! Form a path to get
Mabinni out and then disperse and break up the
crowd. Quickly, or there'll be deaths on both sides!'

The sailors had the advantage of coming from
the backs of the crowd, and the strength of their
discipline to hold them firm against the awesome
heaving and shouting of the throng. And only
seconds later, Mabinni was being rushed by two
of the policemen down the line and into his car.
There was a cut on his cheek and dirt on his white
linen suit. But, to the acute disgust of Engineering
Mechanic Cutler, on the end of the line, he was
alive.

But, when the crowd was finally scattered, two
men were not. And, Boswall noted, neither wore a
Mabinni band.

He looked around. The arrested Crusader,
who had been handcuffed to a rail during the fight,
was using his free hand to stem the blood from a
gash on his neck. And the senior police officer, approaching Boswall, was bleeding beneath an eye.
But, thank God, the ship's company appeared to
be nursing nothing worse than bruises.

'Thank you, sir,' the officer said, saluting.

'Why,' Boswall flared, 'couldn't you have had

more policemen here? We're lucky there weren't dozens of innocent people killed!'

'I agree, sir. But I'm afraid that we have only twelve policemen on Mongada. Seven in the town and five in the villages.' And quietly: 'We did have fifteen, of course, before these troubles began.'

Boswall nodded. 'I'm sorry,' he apologised. 'One tends to forget that this isn't London.'

'In London,' reflected the officer, 'the Crusaders could never threaten an election. But here . . . it's not unlike your I.R.A. problem, but without an army to combat it; just a vastly outnumbered police force.'

'But the Crusaders can't win,' Boswall suggested, 'because the people will automatically choose Loalla?'

'Perhaps, now that we've seen the Crusaders resisted, and beaten by the Navy. But if your ship hadn't come in . . . other republics in the Caribbean and in Central and South America have suffered the same kind of power struggle—and violence has always been a key factor in it. If voting Mabinni in, and appeasing the Crusaders, will stop that violence, then a lot of people must find that a persuasive argument.'

Boswall looked at the policeman. 'Forgive a personal question, but your English is excellent and . . .'

'My penchant for philosophy?' the officer supplied. 'I'm a qualified barrister, Lieutenant, and I was a practising one—until the Crusaders blew up my premises. I decided to join the police force and fight them. One day, when they've been swept off the island, I may start to rebuild my life.'

'How strong *are* the Crusaders?'

'The question is *who* are the Crusaders. The men here today with the armbands—but they claim to be Free Socialists. And who else? One's neighbour? Men in the Government offices who will know, and can let the Crusaders know, who went against Mabinni?' He smiled. 'You've given the people a reason for hope, Lieutenant, where there was none. You've shown that the Crusaders are not all-powerful. Now we must hold the Crusaders down until tomorrow night, to make sure that hope stays with the people until they've signed their voting-slips.'

'They'll suffer for this!' Mabinni raged, pacing his lounge and kicking at the furniture in his usual way. 'By God, they'll suffer!'

'It could have been worse,' volunteered Virgil. 'We were humiliated; we could have been killed. If it hadn't been for the Navy, we would . . .'

'If it hadn't been for the Navy, we'd have crushed Mongada by now! Well, we'll have the Navy fixed by the morning and that gives us the whole of Election Day to remind these *peasants* who runs this island! But we'll start tonight. Tell them to blow up that coffee warehouse in Carron Street!'

'If you're sure you're thinking straight,' agreed Virgil. 'But I'd rather wait until we've had a couple of beers and calmed down. Before we issue *any* orders.'

Mabinni stared wild-eyed, shaking in his fury.

'I told you to . . . you want me to rip you *apart*, Virgil?'

'No, Boss. I want you to be president of Mongada. And I *don't* want you to throw everything away with one angry decision. Maybe you're right. Maybe we should blow the warehouse. But I'd prefer to know that you really mean it before I let the Crusaders loose.'

'All right!' Mabinni fought with himself, and with his temper, then gave himself a cigarette and blew out smoke in a long-drawn sigh. 'O.K., O.K. It's vanity, Virgil. Vanity. I've been insulted by them and I want to hit at them.'

Virgil scratched in relief. 'Let's do one thing at a time. We'll get the Navy's hands tied, and then we'll see to the town.'

'We'll see to it,' Mabinni promised. 'And with the Navy out of the way, God help anyone who tries to stop us!'

Monty Wakelin tapped out a tattoo on Beaumont's door, pushed in and said gaily: 'All right if I have a sub for tonight, Number One?'

Beaumont sat up on his bunk, rubbing his eyes. 'What did you say?'

'Do I have your permission,' Wakelin spelled out, 'to obtain a substitute for my duty this evening? I wish to go ashore.'

'And you woke me up just to ask that? Couldn't it have waited?'

'No,' said the impenitent Wakelin. 'And anyway, it's ten to five. They'll be clearing away tea in a minute, and then you'll moan at the stewards because you dipped out on the sticky buns.'

'I don't moan at the stewards. And I don't need your bloody sticky buns. I need sleep.' He yawned, as if to prove his point. 'Why the urge to get ashore?'

'The usual urge.'

Beaumont grimaced. 'Don't you ever think of your wife, Monty?'

'All the time. I even keep in practice while I'm away.'

'Very funny!' Beaumont got up and splashed water on his face. 'Very well. I don't approve, you may as well know that. But if you can find anyone to be an accessory to your crime, you can go.'

'Thank you, sir!' Wakelin grinned. 'And I promise to reform. As soon as we get back to Devonport!'

'I hope your . . . just a minute!' Beaumont looked at him over the top of his towel. 'You stayed onboard all last night and you've been duty all today. You don't want to get off to try and *find* a girl, do you?'

'Certainly not. I have an appointment.' Wakelin was mock-affronted. 'You don't seem to realise that they come to *me*. Like the glorious Mirabel Parades. She asked my name before she left, I told her I was Lord Wakelin and this afternoon, she rang up and asked me to have dinner with her. A little nibble at her place, you might say!'

'But . . . she's one of *them*!'

'I'm not religious,' Wakelin assured him. 'If it's got bumps on the front and it dances backwards, I'll forgive it almost anything.'

'Don't you . . .'

'Yes! All right! Maybe some guy's going to step from behind the bedroom curtains with a camera. Who cares? I'll order a dozen prints and flog them around the mess-decks! At worst . . .'

'You won't, because you're not going.'

'Oh, come on! I can look after myself!'

'Tell that to the captain.' Beaumont was putting on his jacket.

'What?'

'Look, you twerp. If you took your mind off that bird's bristols long enough to think, it would dawn on even your feeble brain that they could be setting you up for a kidnap!'

'*Could* be. But it's a damned sight more likely that she wants a good time with a randy seafarer —and I'll take the risk.' He grinned irrepressibly. 'All the risks!'

'Tell that to the captain, too. Let's go.'

Wakelin was horrified. 'You want me to tell the captain I've been trying to get a bit out of watch?'

'It won't worry *him*,' Beaumont returned obliquely.

'Eh?'

'Move!' Beaumont smiled grimly. 'It's time the captain knew that there are some dangerous women in this port!'

12

An Assignation

'Wait here,' Beaumont told Wakelin, outside the captain's cabin. He knocked and went in.

Fiona looked up from a book. She smiled: 'It's all right, Derek, the captain hasn't changed shape! He's sleeping.'

'I see,' Beaumont said stonily.

She hesitated. 'I have permission to be here.'

'I'm *sure* you do.' He started across the cabin, and checked as she spoke again.

'Is it important? I think he really is tired.'

Beaumont's jaw knotted. 'We're *all* tired, Miss Hunt. Of one thing or another. And unless you have any prior claim, may *I* be the judge of whether or not he should be woken on ship's business?'

'I'm sorry,' softly. 'I didn't mean to interfere.'

'In his ship,' Beaumont smiled icily, 'or in his life? Or did you borrow the cabin to write to your fiancé?'

'I haven't forgotten that I'm engaged, Derek. Nor has the captain.'

'I hope not.' He turned away, knocked on the sleeping-cabin door and went in.

Nialls opened his eyes. 'Hello, Derek. Excitement?'

'Could be, sir. I think we may have uncovered a possible kidnap attempt. I'd like a word with you, with the Supply Officer present.'

'Fine.' Nialls got off the bunk, pulled a dressing-gown over his shirt and trousers and went through into the day-cabin. 'Sorry, Fiona. Can I have it back for five minutes? Use the sleeping-cabin.'

'Of course, Captain.' She smiled, but he had noticed the brightness in her eyes, and marked her use of 'Captain'. Formality for Beaumont's benefit, or more? It would have to wait.

He closed the door behind her, called: 'Come in, Monty,' then asked: 'What's the score?'

Beaumont told him, not sparing Wakelin's embarrassment, and concluded: 'I wouldn't try to minimise the supply officer's attraction to women, but it sounds likely to me that he would have a gun put to his head and you would get a note saying that they'd pull the trigger if you didn't stop all leave tomorrow.'

'I agree,' Nialls said. 'But you don't, Monty?'

Wakelin swallowed. 'I . . . I thought . . . I was willing to risk it, sir. She seemed genuinely interested in me at the gangway and . . .'

'It might be that,' Nialls grinned at Wakelin, conscious of the lieutenant's discomfort, 'but it's also the logical thing for Mabinni to try next. And I wonder if we shouldn't oblige him.'

'Sir?' from Beaumont.

'Look at it this way.' Nialls lit a cigarette and passed his box to the other two. 'Mabinni is going to try *something* on us. He's got to. But if we deny him his kidnap scheme—assuming it *is* his scheme —he'll have to take another tack, and we may not be ready for it.'

'But if we give him Monty,' Beaumont retorted, 'he's got us. Or Monty gets killed.'

'He'll *think* he's got us,' Nialls conceded. 'But let's say Monty does get kidnapped tonight. They make contact and tell me that I'm not to land sailors tomorrow. I agree. But only on the understanding that in the morning, before I cancel leave, I'll get evidence that Monty's still alive. And we'll have come through the night without any other form of attack.'

Beaumont nodded. 'But what happens to Monty?'

'It all depends on whether Monty's *still* willing to take that risk.' Nialls looked at his supply officer. 'If you are, we can have you followed tonight when you go to the girl's home—say by Last and Fuller, both in plain clothes—and they'll keep track of you until daybreak. Then, if you haven't reappeared with a look of complete satisfaction, we contact Inspector Perdomo and go in and get you.'

'It's too risky!' stressed Beaumont. 'If anything went wrong, Monty would . . .'

'It's less risky than taking this scheme away from Mabinni and waiting to see what he does next. Because the chances are that he'll kidnap a sailor off the streets and we won't have a bloody clue where he is!' Nialls glanced at Wakelin. 'Well, Monty?'

But before Wakelin could reply, Beaumont cut in again: 'Sir, if you insist on this—and I'm strongly against it—then I have a better idea. Monty's a married man and I'm not. I'll ring the Parades girl, tell her that Monty's duty—which she knows—but that I'll come instead.'

'Not on.' Nialls was emphatic. 'Thanks for the offer, Derek. But if Mabinni knows that Monty's talked about this, he'll guess that we've rumbled it. Monty has to assure the girl that *no one* else knows where he is. He's a married man with a staid old captain and first lieutenant and he's sneaked ashore to her without telling anyone where he's going.'

Wakelin cleared his throat noisily.

'Yes, Monty?'

'I'll go, sir.' He tried a smile, which failed. 'I won't pretend that you haven't both put the fear of God into me, but you're right. If we don't go for this, he *will* do something else that we know nothing about.' Another attempt at a smile. 'I hope she cooks a good dinner!'

Nialls looked at him. 'Thanks, Monty.'

Beaumont was still unhappy. 'I have to say, sir, that it's out of our field. And if it *has* to be done, can we get a policeman in on it from the start? And can I go? Instead of Last.'

'All right. You go with Fuller. I'll have to stay onboard now, at any rate. And I'll see if I can get Inspector Perdomo himself. I'm sure that all his officers are reliable, but if we're playing with Monty's safety we can't take the chance that one of his men *could* be a Crusader. Will you send up the car, to ask if he can come and see me at his early convenience?'

'Aye aye, sir.' Beaumont rose.

'And you, Monty, had better break out your best after-shave. And take your toothbrush, since you may be staying the night!'

When they had both gone, Nialls sat for a moment, wondering what he had done. He had thrown a terrible burden on Wakelin's young shoulders, and taken a terrible risk with his life. Beaumont was right about that. But Mabinni was bound to go for a kidnap; it was the only conceivable lever by which the ship's company could be separated from the town. And it was better to stage a kidnap *for* Mabinni than let him choose his own.

He hoped. And prayed.

And was still hoping when Dancer knocked on the door.

'Telegram for Miss Hunt, sir.'

'Thank you, Yeoman.'

It was addressed 'CARE OF COMMANDING OFFICER WARSHIP HERO' and read:

PLEASE ADVISE DATE AND METHOD YOUR RETURN ENGLAND. WILL MEET YOU. MISSING YOU AND LOVING YOU. NAT.

Nialls got up, went into the sleeping-cabin and eased to silence: Fiona was asleep on the bunk. He drew close and looked down on her; on the golden hair spilled upon the pillow, the composed face with its haunting beauty, the young and exciting figure arched in sleep against her dress.

He stood for a time, gazing at her with a wealth of yearning in his heart; and with renewed resolve.

It must not be. At least, not this time around. He had to accept that. She belonged to another man, another generation, another world. She had much to learn; and it was better that she learned *with* her Nat, rather than *from* a man called Mark Nialls, who was too far along the road to go back and walk it again, with her. He would want to hurry her along, skip her past essential milestones of experience, and the gap was simply too wide. Sixteen years too wide.

She had to make the long crawl, and make it for herself. At her own pace. In her own time. And with a rightful travelling companion.

Commander, he told himself, you are in an out-of-bounds area. He smiled sadly and returned to the day-cabin, to pour himself a drink.

And we are the dreamers of dreams . . .

As he finished the drink, Boswall came to report on the incident at the football ground, and on later and more minor incidents in the town, and to say that he had now taken over as officer of the day from Wakelin, who wanted to go ashore.

Nialls walked with Boswall back to the flight deck and telephoned Roberts at the embassy. Roberts said that they would be delighted to accommodate Fiona; Janet had liked her. Was everything else all right?

Nialls assured him that it was, thanked him again and hung up as Inspector Perdomo came over the gangway. They went together to the cabin and when Perdomo had a gin and tonic in his hand, Nialls told him what he proposed to do in respect of Wakelin.

'It's playing for high stakes,' said the policeman, sipping at his drink. 'I agree with your reasoning, and it's sensible if Wakelin's willing to take the chance, but these things can go very wrong.'

'I accept that. And the responsibility for it. Will you be able to accompany my men?'

'Willingly.' Perdomo smiled. 'I owe you a favour: your men probably saved the lives of mine today, at Mabinni's rally.'

'Yes, I heard. Glad we could help.' Nialls paused. 'What do you know of Mirabel Parades? Is there any possibility that she's genuinely interested in Wakelin? That we could be misreading the whole situation—which would give the advantage back to Mabinni?'

Perdomo shrugged expressively. 'Who can tell with girls, these days? But she's trusted by Mabinni: apart from being his messenger today, she went with him to Nassau, to what we believe was a Crusaders' convention. Although as far as I know, he hasn't used her much since.' He laughed. 'Perhaps, what would you say . . . her performance does not measure up to her looks? Your man Wakelin could be in for a disappointing night!'

'As long as he survives it,' said Nialls, as a heart-felt prayer.

Perdomo left the ship at seven-twenty-five, Fuller at seven-thirty in the car, and Beaumont at seven-forty. Fuller drove to a side-street near the address given him by Wakelin at their final briefing, then left the car and took up station opposite the smart, modern apartment building which Mirabel had

claimed as her home. Perdomo and Beaumont
joined up in the shadows at the end of the jetty and
at seven minutes to eight, Wakelin walked past
them and turned up towards the town and his fate.
He stayed on foot, to facilitate his followers, and
made the climb to Mirabel's address on legs that
had in them an annoying tremble, to remind him of
the nature of his mission. And the tremble increased
alarmingly as he pressed the bell of Flat 5.

The door opened on Mirabel's full-strength
smile. 'Monty! Come in!'

She was wearing a black dress with a halter neck
that plunged to her waist and proffered a mind-
bending display of warm, honey-coloured flesh
that begged to be touched and stroked. And for a
moment, Wakelin's trembling was of a different
kind.

She led him into a dining-room, where a table
was set with two places for dinner, and his optim-
ism increased still further when she asked: 'What
would you like to drink? I'm on rum and coke.'

'I'd be happy with that,' he said, and heard the
dryness of his throat rasp into his speech. But his
throat would have been dry anyway, he reflected.
He was revealing nothing of his fear there.

She gave him his drink and a chair, then settled
herself opposite him and probed: 'Did you have
any trouble getting off your duty?'

'No, I told them that I'd a dinner invitation from
a member of the embassy staff. That impressed
my snobby first lieutenant and he let me go.'

'Don't you have to leave an address when you
come off the ship?'

'Not on night leave. No one knows *where* I am.'

She laughed. 'Come now, I know what men are like! Are you trying to tell me that you resisted the temptation of telling your friends that you'd found a girl? No winks in the mess, bets on how you'd do?'

'Are you kidding? I'm married. Sometimes. And our first lieutenant is a prude as well as a snob. If I advertised my . . . success ashore, I'd be ruining my career.' The captain had been right, he thought. She wanted to be sure of his discretion. He obliged: 'I've learned to keep my mouth shut in that ship.'

Her smile widened and she began to play with the neck of her dress, running her fingers down the inside of it. In a teasing note, she queried: 'Are you hungry yet?'

'Only for you.'

'Good.' She drifted to her feet. 'Wait here.'

She moved to the bedroom, pushed the door wide and said: 'He's yours!'

And two men stepped past her with guns in their hands. They were Negroes; and huge.

Christ, Wakelin decided, this is it. His heart was pounding as he sprang to his feet and lifted his hands. At least, he did not have to act scared—he was petrified.

He looked to the girl. 'You're wasting your time, Mirabel. I've no money.'

'Shut up,' commanded one of the men. He crossed to Wakelin, eased behind him and searched him for weapons. Then his gun went into Wake-

lin's back. 'We're goin' for a li'l ride, Lootenant.
And you're goin' to be a good li'l baby!'

Mirabel smiled. 'Bye bye, Monty. Have fun.'

Wakelin wondered if he ought to protest, concluded that it would do no harm and demanded:
'What's this all about? You've got the wrong fellow!'

'No talking,' instructed the second man, who was
smaller than his companion—Wakelin thought—
only inasmuch as full-grown gorillas can come in
different sizes. 'We go.'

They went, leaving Mirabel at the telephone.
And as they emerged from the front door of the
building and walked to a nearby car, Perdomo whispered: 'It's the car, gentlemen. I'll drive. Be ready
for a run to it when I give the word.'

Beaumont tensed. The chase was on. He hoped
to God that Nialls had made the right decision.

And that Wakelin would keep his nerve.

'Got him,' Mirabel said into the telephone. 'He's
on his way to the Avenue.'

'Did you check him out?' Mabinni countered.
'He didn't give anyone the address or . . .'

'He didn't tell anyone *anything*.' She laughed.
'He was worried about his career!'

'Right. Get out of there and go home. You know
where to return the flat keys?'

'Yes, but couldn't I come and see you? Tonight?'

A pause. 'Why not? We'll be celebrating shortly.'

'That'll be nice,' she told him.

Perdomo kept the car well behind their quarry,

speeding up only when the other had turned a corner. He said: 'They're not going to Mabinni's. Although I didn't expect them to. We'd never prove an involvement with him. The girl will be paid to say that she was working independently of him. She may hint at a Crusader involvement, but we'll get nothing more.'

'I don't think we care,' Beaumont responded, his eyes on the car ahead, 'if we can get through the night without further trouble and we can bring Wakelin clear in the morning.'

'That's the important thing,' agreed Fuller from the back seat. 'It must be hell for the captain, having to wait and not knowing what's going on.'

'Yes,' Beaumont said. And thought acidly: except that he has other things to fill his mind.

'Have you something on your mind?' Fiona asked, across the dinner-table in the cabin.

'Not much,' denied Nialls. 'Why?'

'You're not eating. And I'm getting quite jealous of that watch: it seems to have a great attraction for you!'

He smiled. 'Sorry. I'm waiting for a telephone call. Secret lover.'

'Very mysterious.'

'Part of my image. But,' he pointed to the desk, 'I've had the shore 'phone reconnected in here, so that I don't have to leave you to take the call.'

'So that you can get the call quicker,' she amended with a laugh. 'And privately.'

He shook his head in supposed despair. 'Is there no romance in you, Miss Hunt? Is there . . . that reminds me, why were you crying when I woke up this evening; when Derek was here?'

'I wasn't crying.'

'You were damned near to it. And you called me "Captain" rather formally. Has Derek been expressing his disapproval?'

She hesitated. 'He's fond of you. I think he was trying to protect you.'

'Well, he can . . .'

The telephone rang.

Nialls put down his napkin carefully, and got up slowly. It would be wrong to grab for the telephone as soon as it started ringing. He walked to it, sat on a corner of the desk and lifted the receiver. He spoke into it evenly and clearly.

'Commanding officer, HMS *Hero*.'

'Perdomo,' said the strained voice of the policeman. 'We've lost them, Captain.'

13

Scotland the Brave

Nialls' heart churned as his grip on the receiver tightened. He whipped his mind into top gear.

'Did they know they were being followed?'

'No. It was bad luck. Another car reversed into the road from parking, right in front of us. Blocked us out. Innocent driver. But they were away.'

'Look,' Nialls was cold, brittle-voiced, 'they wouldn't deliver a hand-message to the ship, so they have to call me here. Can you get the call traced if I hold on to them for as long as possible?'

'I'm in the telephone-exchange now,' Perdomo said reassuringly. 'But there's no guarantee that they'll call from the same place they're holding Wakelin.'

'There is. I'll insist on speaking to Wakelin, to know that he's still alive. And I'll get as tough with them as I dare, waste as much time as I can. They need me more than I need them—Mabinni can't afford to lose this one.'

'It's Wakelin's life.'

'Inspector, the only way to save his life is to trace that call. If we don't get him back in the morning, they'll kill him in the end—come what may—to protect their organisation.'

'Right,' agreed Perdomo. 'I'll ring off and we'll be ready. Give me as much time as you can, but please don't get them suspicious!'

'Understood.'

Nialls replaced the receiver with an air of re-signed decision as the girl queried softly: 'Have they got Lieutenant Wakelin?'

'We gave them Lieutenant Wakelin,' he said. 'Now, it's a question of whether or not we can get him back.'

'What . . . I don't follow.'

'Never mind. It's not your problem. I'll get some one to take you to the embassy.'

'Mark, *please* tell me. Don't leave it at that.'

He looked at her, reading her distress in the lovely face, and relented: 'All right, since you know half of it already. But my ship's company don't know, and no one else is to know.' He told her of the plan, and of the latest development, and ended: 'The difficulty now is to judge how far I can go in time-wasting. If I overplay it, I could scare them off. But this call is my only real chance. It's sure to be the longest of any they make, because they have to explain their proposition and I can legiti-mately challenge and query and play stunned. Any later calls will be a hell of a lot shorter, and if we don't get them this time and they move him in the night, we start from square one again next time with the odds really against us.'

Fiona's eyes mirrored her shock. 'Darling, I'm

so sorry for you! Poor Lieutenant Wakelin. And you must feel . . .'

'Spare me the sympathy, Fiona! Perdomo warned me that it could go wrong, I accepted that and I'll accept whatever comes from it. You'll go back to flying, won't you?'

'Yes, of course, it's my job.'

'And I'll go on taking decisions and standing by them. That's *my* job.' He reached for the internal telephone. 'Now, I'll fix for you to be taken home.'

'I'd rather stay with you.'

'No,' he said firmly, 'I'll see this night through on my own. I'll call you in the morning.'

She came to him. 'Mark, I know there's nothing I can do, but . . . wouldn't it help if I stayed? I'd never want you to be alone. Feel alone.'

Their hands touched and he drew her to him and looked down into the blue, concerned eyes. And the spell was on him again as he lifted a hand into the golden hair and brought her mouth to his. For a moment, as before, time stood still and then he broke away and lifted the 'phone, calling the flight deck.

'Quartermaster? Captain. Is Lieutenant Last still onboard? Good. Send him to me at once. Thanks.'

'Mark . . .'

'No, Fiona! I'm juggling with a man's life. I can't allow . . . our magic to intervene tonight.'

She nodded reluctantly. 'But you *will* ring me in the morning? Tell me if everything's come right?'

'I promise.' He smiled. 'How's your pulse-rate?'

'I'd fail a flying medical. Do you always kiss girls like that?'

'Not often. Must look after my heart.'

'I've lost mine,' she said steadily.

And he was saved from committing himself in reply by a knock on the door.

'Come in!'

Last entered. 'You sent for me, sir?'

'Pilot, I want you to draw a pistol and ammunition. Then take Miss Hunt to the embassy in a taxi. And if you're stopped, or hazarded in any way, shoot first and sort it out afterwards. That's an order.'

'Aye aye, sir.' Last was mystified. 'Are we expecting anything . . . special?'

'No,' Nialls was grim-faced, 'but then we weren't expecting anything special last night, and we damned nearly had the ship blown out from under us. So you will take no chances.'

'I understand, sir.'

'I hope you do.' And Nialls added thoughtfully: 'Remember that things can go wrong when you *least* expect it.'

The telephone rang again at nine-fifty-five. Nialls answered it in the same manner as before, and a voice said: 'Evenin', Captain. This is the Caribbean People's Crusaders Organisation.'

'I have nothing to say to you,' Nialls retorted pompously.

'I guess you have, Captain. We're holdin' Lootenant Montgomery Charles Wakelin.'

'What? What for?'

'But can't you guess, Captain? It's simple. You stop all leave tomorrow, and we'll send your boy back to you tomorrow night. You got that?'

Nialls touched anger into his voice. 'What makes you think you can blackmail the Royal Navy?'

'This gun I'm holdin', Captain. It's pointin' at your boy's head.'

A pause; Nialls lit a cigarette.

'You still there, Captain? I haven't all night.'

'What guarantee have I that he'll ever be returned?'

'None, Captain. We don't give guarantees. We're not that kind of firm.'

Nialls took a deep breath. 'Then I'm not doing business with you. Good night.'

'*Hold it!* You can talk to him now. And again in the mornin'. How's that?'

'Not good enough. I talk to him now, at eight in the morning, again at midday and at eight tomorrow night, you release him. The election will be over then and there's no need for you to hold him after that.'

'O.K., Captain. Now, eight in the mornin' and midday. We're reasonable people. I'll put him on now. He can tell you that we aren't playin' games, all the same.'

'One moment!' Nialls' eyes were on his watch. 'I don't have very much to do with Wakelin. He's only a lieutenant. I'm not sure that I'll know him by his voice. I must have time to question him, satisfy myself that it's really him.'

Damn, Nialls thought. That did not sound convincing; and if his caller knew anything about the

Navy, he would know that Wakelin, as a head of department, saw and spoke with his captain daily.

But the man said: 'Sure, sure. Two questions, two answers. Nice, short ones. He isn't very bright tonight.'

Wakelin came on the line. 'Hello, sir? Sir, I've been kidnapped!'

'So I hear, Monty, but don't worry. We'll make sure you aren't harmed. Now, please give me the answers to a couple of questions, just to make sure we're on the same wavelength. What's the name of the first lieutenant?'

'Derek Beaumont.'

'And the leading regulator?'

'Fuller. Pat Fuller.'

'Glad you haven't forgotten them,' Nialls said pointedly. 'Keep your chin up and . . .'

'O.K., Captain,' the other voice, 'save the love and kisses. He's alive and he'll stay that way if you're smart. We'll be on again at eight, and at noon. But be waitin'. We know you can't be tracin' this call on another line, because you've only *got* one line into the shore-exchange. At the moment. But you could have that changed by the mornin', so the next calls are goin' to be real money-savin' ones. One question, one answer. And we don't even give time to say goodbye. You got that, too?'

'I'll be here.'

'Right. And one other thing, Captain. This is a private arrangement. But strictly private. No cops, no consul, no president. If it leaks out why you're co-operatin', he dies just the same. See?'

Another pause.

'You with all that, Captain?'

'I've got it. And you can tell Mabinni that I'll get *him*.'

'Mabinni? Who's that?' A laugh, and the line went dead.

Nialls hung up and sank into his chair. He prayed that Perdomo, Beaumont and Fuller were now racing for an address in the town. And he hoped that one of them, at some time, would remember to call him with the news.

Mabinni looked at the poster, its print still wet. It said:

PEOPLE OF MONGADA

You will see that there are no British sailors in the streets today. And you will wonder why. The answer is that they have been ordered to remain in their ship, rather than face the Crusaders. Even the British Navy now acknowledges the might of our Organisation for Freedom.

The Crusaders support the Free Socialist Party of Mongada, as the true instrument of freedom on this island. You must support it, too. For enemies of the Crusaders will be vanquished, as the British Navy has been, and a vote for the tyranny of Loalla is a warrant for death.

VOTE TODAY

VOTE FOR STRENGTH

VOTE FOR MABINNI

'I like it,' Mabinni said. 'Not bad at all, for a rush job!'

Virgil nodded. 'They'll be put up all over town by early morning and handed out in the streets and at polling-stations during the day.'

Mirabel Parades rubbed herself against Mabinni's arm. 'Congratulations, Mr President.'

Mabinni hugged her. 'Maybe it's too soon for that. But we're back in with a fighting chance. Get the scotch out, Virgil. The toast is *Election Day!*'

Nialls had not moved from the telephone, and the silence in the cabin had been broken only by Last's return to report the safe delivery of Fiona.

At least, he consoled himself, Perdomo must have had some measure of success: if they had failed to trace the call, he would have rung ere now. But if the Crusaders had moved immediately after telephoning . . .

There was no reason why they should have done that. It would be a risk for them to take Wakelin out on the streets again. But . . .

The telephone shrilled impatiently.

He snatched it up. 'Nialls.'

'Fuller, sir. We've got them again. Address is 7 Balinna Avenue. Lights are on and their car's outside.'

'Does the inspector want any more men?'

'No, sir. I asked about that. He's got a gun and he reckons on going in at dawn.'

'How many Crusaders are in the house?'

'Just two, as far as we know. The girl didn't go with them.'

Nialls thought for a moment. 'Fuller, suggest to the inspector that when he's ready to go in, you should come down the street singing and shouting and try to get into their car. If you make enough racket, one of them will come out to tell you to clear off. That's going to get the door open for the inspector and the men separated.'

'Right, sir.'

'And encourage Perdomo to use the gun if he has to. I want Lieutenant Wakelin out in one piece.'

'We'll make sure of that, sir.'

'Just make sure you ring me as soon as he's free. My hair's turning grey, second by second.'

'Roger, sir.'

Fuller rang off and Nialls sat back. It was going to be *another* long night.

With the first streaks of dawn, Fuller loosed himself on the slumbering Balinna Avenue, staggering from side to side of the street and singing a raucous mixture of *Scotland the Brave* and *Land of Hope and Glory*. Perdomo and Beaumont were crouched on either side of the door to Number 7, and Perdomo's revolver was cocked.

'*Land of the high endeavour*,' bawled Fuller and then stopped, swaying, to inspect the car. He kicked affectionately at its tyres, then walked solemnly around it, trying all the doors.

All were locked; and this discovery was the prompt, apparently, for an ear-splitting burst of '*God who made her mighty*' as he shifted his attentions to the bonnet. He lifted it and ducked beneath to examine the engine; and as he did so—he noted from the corner of an eye—a curtain parted at the lighted window of the house.

And suddenly, the front door opened and the smaller Crusader roared blindly out past Perdomo and Beaumont and to the car. He, too, ducked beneath the bonnet and he pushed his face into Fuller's, demanding: 'What the hell are you doing, fella?'

Fuller whipped out from under the bonnet, knocked the man over the engine and slammed down the lid, throwing his weight on it. And at once, Perdomo sprang into the house with Beaumont at his heels, across a small hallway and into a lighted lounge, where the bigger Crusader was turning from the window, a pistol in his hand. Perdomo shot him unhesitatingly through the heart, glanced at the dazed and seated Wakelin and ran out again into the street.

The other Crusader had fought his way from under the bonnet and was now clubbing at Fuller with the barrel of his revolver. Fuller staggered back, the gun came up and a shot rang out.

The Crusader half-spun to Perdomo's bullet, clutched at his head and fell to Fuller's feet. Fuller hurdled the still-rolling body and raced for the housedoor.

'Take it easy,' Beaumont told him, having come from a search of the other rooms. 'The game's over.'

Together, they went into the lounge and to a relieved, white-faced Wakelin.

'Hello, sir,' Fuller greeted, surprised at the tremor in his own voice, 'have a good run ashore?'

'I don't know,' said Wakelin, 'that I'll ever manage another. I don't think I can get off this chair. I need a drink before I try to stand up.'

Fuller coughed. 'If the first lieutenant would kindly look the other way.' He handed across a small hip-flask. 'Rum, sir. Pink gin's off today.'

Beaumont half-smiled tiredly and stilled a shudder as his eyes fell on the body of the Crusader, beneath the window. He lit a cigarette to take the smell of death from his nostrils and looked to Perdomo, on the telephone to Nialls.

'Captain, we made it.'

In his cabin, Nialls closed his eyes and thanked all the gods. 'Well done, Inspector. Is everyone all right?'

'Everyone. Apart from the Crusaders. They're both dead.'

'Good.' And Nialls meant it. He was drained, and in no mood of forgiveness. 'I think I may grant leave even earlier this morning. No reason why the boys shouldn't discover what a Mongadian breakfast is like, before they go to the polls.'

Perdomo laughed. 'That appeals to me. I'll come and see you now. I'd like to talk about the deployment of our men to cover the polling-stations and also some of the factories the Crusaders have named as targets.'

'Be my guest,' Nialls invited. 'No reason why *you* should have a Mongadian breakfast! And I want to see you anyway: if you can give my flight commander the exact locations of the rural stations, we'll see that some of our lads are dropped off around those.'

'Excellent, Captain! I have a feeling that it could be a glorious day. But not for Mabinni!'

Mabinni awakened to the crash of Virgil's coming through his bedroom door. He rolled away from Mirabel Parades and sat up.

'What the . . .'

'Sailors!' Virgil panted. 'All over the town. All over the island. And that lieutenant's gone. And Bud and Benny are dead!'

Mabinni reeled. 'Can't be! How . . .'

'What is it, Raoul?' asked Mirabel.

'Out!' Mabinni commanded. 'Get out and shut up!'

'But,' she was clutching the sheet to her breast, 'I'm . . . would you mind, Virgil?'

'Out!' Mabinni roared again, grabbing her and hurling her naked body to the floor. 'Clear off and make some coffee! And *you*,' a scream at Virgil, 'stop gaping and for Christ's sake, tell me what's *happened*!'

'Been trying to piece it together from other people who live in the Avenue. Sounds like Nialls knew from the beginning what we were doing: two of his men went in with Perdomo and snatched the lieutenant.'

'Check reports?'

Virgil was unhappy. 'They were normal. Nialls didn't put his men in until first light.'

'That *bitch*!' Mabinni, also naked, was out of bed and shaking in raw fury, his face contorted and his hands claw-like and quivering. 'She told me that Nialls didn't know. Said she'd checked it. I'll kill her! She's thrown it all away!'

'It wasn't . . .' Virgil began and was smashed aside by Mabinni.

'It was!' Mabinni was worse than even Virgil had ever seen him. 'Oh God! Those posters! Those damned posters! What has she *done* to us? "No British sailors in the streets today". "Vote for strength." Oh, no! *No!*'

Mabinni tore at his hair, then screamed anew and rushed into the kitchen, where Mirabel—now dressed in a loose, open shirt—was at the sink. He caught her by the hair, twisted it and pulled her backwards to him. 'You bitch!' he repeated. 'The posters! The whole island will be laughing at them. Showing them to sailors!'

'Raoul!' It was a shriek. 'Raoul, I . . .'

And then a sob, choked-off and horrible.

And Mabinni looked down at the kitchen knife which had come into his hand, and at the ugly hole —welling red—between her breasts. He dropped the knife and allowed the girl to fall; then turned to face a horrified Virgil.

Mabinni passed him, went through to the bedroom and fell upon the bed, burying his face in the pillow. In a low, muffled and broken voice, he asked: 'What hope is there, Virgil? What hope?'

'We've lost, boss. That was the last throw.'

Then he stretched a hairy hand to Mabinni's bare shoulder and said quietly: 'Come on, boss. We've got to play it through. We'd better go and vote.'

14

Angel of the Morning

Beaumont came into Nialls' cabin as Perdomo left, and said: 'Will you be taking defaulters today, sir? You should really see Able Seaman Regard.'

'Did he plead guilty at your investigation?'

'Yes—offered in mitigation that he was very tired, having been up all of the previous night. But no attempt to excuse himself.'

Nialls nodded. 'I should hang him, by rights. But if he hadn't been sleeping, and Fuller hadn't taken the rifle . . . he's a bachelor?'

'Yes. A fine?'

'I think so, in all the circumstances. Agree?'

'I do, sir.' Beaumont was being his correct self again. 'On another matter, sir: Pilot's cleared for us to sail at oh-eight-hundred in the morning. If that's convenient.'

'Convenient to me.' Nialls smiled. 'Think you'll get the stragglers back by then? If Loalla wins the election—and I can't see him losing now—the boys are going to be feted ashore tonight.'

'I'm sure *they* will make it, sir.'

Nialls sighed. 'All right. Get it off your chest.'

'I beg your pardon, sir?'

'You want to say,' Nialls anticipated, 'that you disapprove of my . . . seeing Miss Hunt.'

'It's not for me to approve or disapprove. But . . .'

'But you see her as some kind of Lolita. She's engaged to be married and soon, she'll go back to England and to her fiancé. But in the meantime, she's set her sights on the captain of *Hero* and the poor old boy is bound to have his heart broken by her. Yes?'

Beaumont hesitated. 'I wouldn't have put it in precisely those terms, sir. But leaving aside her engagement, she's rather too young *and* too beautiful. It's a combination that makes a schoolgirl-crush rather more dangerous than endearing. And "Lolita" is *your* word, not mine.'

'Derek, I'm not encouraging a crush; merely enjoying the company of an unusual girl who's— unfortunately—almost young enough to be my daughter. In the short time I've known her, I've come to love her very much. But she's *in love* with her lad in England, and that's the way it's going to stay.' He smiled. 'Thanks for the friendly word, though—it *might* have been needed.'

'I apologise, sir,' genuinely. 'To you both.' Beaumont grinned, gathered up his papers and left.

And Nialls lit a cigarette and kept his smile. The hell of it was that Beaumont *was* being loyal: he had recognised the lorelei, read the warning beacons and analysed the danger—Fiona was all too different.

Nialls had called her at the embassy before breakfast, as he had promised, and invited her to bring Janet and Stan Roberts to lunch onboard. She had been youthfully jubilant at the news of Wakelin's escape; and thoughtfully mature about the effect of the night on Nialls. And perhaps that was one key to her fascination: she had a great love of life, yet a deep concern for it. An effervescent enthusiasm, yet a sympathetic sensitivity. A beauty to outshine the day, yet a humbleness to weep away the night.

Nialls had told her that his recuperation demanded no more than early sight of her and she had promised to bring Bayldon, who was leaving the island in the afternoon, to say goodbye during the morning.

Now, he was impatient to see her again and had sent Last with the car to collect her and Bayldon. Otherwise, his day was well ordered: the Roberts and Fiona for lunch; an afternoon tour of the polling-stations with Perdomo; and in the evening, for captain and officers, an 'at-home' with the Loallas —sure now to be a victory celebration.

And in the morning, they would sail. As they had done so many times before. But this time, despite his resolutions, something of him must remain. Something of him would dwell forever in this sun-baked, violence-scarred island.

It was the business of the posters which had finally beaten the Crusaders. It was impossible for them to issue convincing threats in the face of the ridicule heaped upon them by the poster-waving crowds; and after a few early and minor scuffles, there was little evidence of the Free Socialist Party.

With Mabinni's acceptance of defeat, and withdrawal from the role of their commander-in-chief, the Crusaders were denied the driving force and the cohesion for telling influence; and not even the gunmen could be tempted into open conflict for what was now patently a lost cause.

The polling-stations were witness to the carnival atmosphere of the town, as people met and chatted and chortled at the posters while shaking sailors by the hand. Only once had real ugliness marred the gaiety of the scene and that was when Mabinni and Virgil arrived at the main polling-station at the Town Hall, to cast their votes. They were met with a deafening cacophony of abuse and booing and—to his heartfelt chagrin—Engineering Mechanic Cutler found himself for a second time in a protective formation around Mabinni.

Then, even that furore had passed; and the celebrations continued. The streets were filled and overspilled by the carousing throngs and it took Last almost an hour to bring Fiona and Bayldon to the ship in the captain's car. But no one minded.

It was becoming that kind of a day.

And thus it remained.

The people voted early, to be free to concentrate on their amusement, and by the time the polls closed at eight o'clock, sufficient results had been tabled to establish a landslide victory for Joshua Loalla. And at eight-fifteen, Raoul Mabinni formally conceded the election.

It was then that the celebrations began in earnest. It was as if the daytime activities had been but a rather half-hearted rehearsal, during which the people had conserved their energies for the nocturnal frolics. The town became a firework-lit backdrop for a colourful mass of singing, dancing and cheering Mongadians; the sailors were dragged into congas in the streets, toasted in the bars, kissed by the girls. And the huge crowd around Government House reserved a special roar for Nialls, brought to the balcony from the party by a beaming, triumphant Loalla.

And Nialls looked down on the sea of happy faces and knew that his battle had been just. And when he was joined by Fiona, again at Loalla's bidding, he took the girl's hand in his own and allowed his gaze to travel beyond the crowd to the lights of HMS *Hero*.

And again, time stood still for him; and he wondered if any man had the right to be so at peace.

He turned to Fiona and smiled to her. Speech was impossible above the clamour from the streets, but it was enough to be with her, to share the moment with her.

She was dressed in a red open-necked shirt and a white pleated skirt and the face beneath the golden hair was lit by the coloured flares of the fireworks, and by her happiness. He had never seen her quite so beautiful; quite so desirable. And this was a night for joy, a night to be stolen from the real world and . . .

Loalla tapped him on the shoulder and led him back inside and to a room off the party, where Roberts and Perdomo were waiting.

The inspector said: 'Mabinni's dead, Captain. We thought you should know.'

'What happened to him?'

'He was hacked to death by machetes, at the entrance to his headquarters. We found Mirabel Parades inside. She'd been stabbed, and dead for some time. I suspect that Mabinni killed her—presumably for the failure of the kidnap.'

Nialls nodded. 'But the Crusaders killed Mabinni?'

'Maybe,' conceded Perdomo. 'Except that the Crusaders have been keeping off the streets today. I'm not sure that he wasn't executed by the will of the people. It's murder, of course, and we'll follow it up; but it'll be difficult when almost every man in the island had the motive to commit the crime.'

'I can't be sorry,' Roberts admitted.

'You mustn't be!' Loalla's gaze embraced them all. 'Not tonight. Tonight's a time for love and laughter and hope, my friends. Tomorrow will come soon enough.'

'It'll soon be tomorrow,' Fiona said from the passenger seat, 'and you'll be gone.'

Nialls smiled as he waited for the crowd to clear a good-humoured path for the car. 'Are you going into a *vin triste*?'

'No! But I want to stay up all night. See the sunrise. From our beach. I've warned Janet and Stan.'

'If that's what you want . . .' Nialls was amused. 'Although I was up all *last* night. I'll probably fall asleep long before sunrise.'

'I won't care,' she said ingenuously, 'if I'm near you. But I'm not going to let you go one minute before I have to. Time's precious to me.'

'And to me, Fiona.' His voice was suddenly quiet. 'But it's impossible to hold up time, in the same way that . . . some dreams are impossible. The secret is to learn to live with that fact; to console oneself in the knowledge that at another time, and another place, it might all have been different.'

'In other words, keep to the rules?'

'That's right.' He had the car moving now. 'And it's important that you do—because I'm no longer sure that I can.'

But he did.

They walked, and talked; smoked cigarettes, and cast pebbles at the moon; watched the sea go out, and start to come in again. The night fled from them. An enchanted, bewitched night that all too soon turned itself into a soft, stealthy dawn.

Nialls followed its climb as it came inch by inch, cloud-rung by cloud-rung, out of the sea and into the sky; then he looked back at the girl—and stared.

She was unbuttoning her shirt.

'What are you doing?' he asked, in some alarm.

'Going for a swim.' That impish grin. 'In my underclothes. Don't panic.'

'But . . . how will you get dry?'

She had stepped out of her skirt. 'I have a handkerchief.' Another grin. 'Are you shocked, Commander Nialls?'

'Stunned.' He was gazing unashamedly on the

magnificence of her figure. And his resolve was melting. He moved towards her, his heart pounding.

And she skipped out of his reach, raced across the sand and plunged into the sea.

He smiled and shook his head as he saw the fair hair lift out of the waves, and he raised a hand in answer to the peal of rich laughter that rolled back to him before she turned and began to strike out strongly for the pale horizon.

Angel of the morning.

She had come to him out of the sea, on a morning that seemed now so very long ago; and in a moment, she would come out of the sea again, and into a new morning. A new day. A new life. A young life.

And he would go back to sea.

And it had to be; for, as he had told her, it was impossible to hold up time.

He smiled again as he watched her turn, outpace the waves to the shore and jump up in the shallows, in a flurry of spray and giggling. She left footprints in the wet sand as she ran to him, and arrived in his arms in a breathless, laughing rush, shouting: 'It's freezing! It's freezing!'

He laughed with her, kissed her nose and hugged her; carried into the game by the momentum of her unquenchable zest for fun, but managing to protest weakly: 'This is like being on a run ashore to Niagara Falls! And are you aware, Miss Hunt, that your underwear becomes transparent when wet?'

'Who cares? You need a shave. And your uniform's getting crumpled and somehow damp!'

She giggled. 'Oh, Captain, you can't return to the ship like that. You'd better desert and stay with me!'

'I couldn't stand the pace,' he said, and hugged her again. 'Come on, we have to go.'

The laughter went from her eyes. 'Already?'

'Yes, Fiona,' gently.

'I don't ever want to go,' she whispered. And her arms went around his neck as she half-turned him to meet her lips. 'I love you, Captain.'

And the shot rang out.

She gave a little gasp and the blue eyes widened questioningly to his face.

As if in a dream, he heard the screech of brakes from the road, and other shots and shouting; but that was in another world.

The bullet had gone through her back and he knew that she had seconds only to cling to that life which she had lived so well. He lowered her tenderly to the sand and cradled her in his arms as he struggled for the words that might convey his last message to her, explain to her all that their stolen time had meant to him, would always mean to him.

But Fiona had found words first and through her pain and her tears, she sobbed: 'You see? We needn't have worried. There *is* a way to end it.'

And he touched his mouth to the now-stilled lips and he could hear her voice again, speaking from the sea. *Their* sea.

'*I don't ever want to go,*' she had said.

And once, a million years before: '*Things passing, disturbing us, moving on, but leaving us never quite the same again. Love and hate. Life and*